The Curse of

the Werck Family

Volume 1

The Battle Between Love and Hate

The Curse of

the Werck Family

Volume 1

The Battle Between Love and Hate

Valéria Lopes

by the spirit Andorra

Copyright © 2016 by Piu Books LLC
1ª Edition – September 2016

Publisher Piu Book
4700 N.W. Boca Raton Blvd, Suite 202
Boca Raton, Florida, US - Zip 33431

Visit our site   **www.piubook.com**

Like our pages on   **www.facebook.com/piubook**
                                     www.instagram.com/piubook
                                     www.twitter.com/@piubook

Talk to us by our e-mail   **pb@piubook.com**

Translation	: Silvia Silva and Mariele Flores
Review	: Patrick Kearney
Cover design by	: Maíra Lopes / Family's Design
Editorial Coordination	: Rosana Lopes

International Data for Cataloging in Publication (ICP)

Lopes, Valéria
    The Curse of the Werck Family – Volume I: The Battle between
Love and Hate / by Valéria Lopes [translated by Silvia Silva and
Mariele Flores]. – 1ed. – Florida: Piu Books LLC, 2016. – (Series
The Curse of the Werck Family, v 1).

Translated from: A Maldição dos Werck: A Batalha entre o Amor
e o Ódio.

ISBN 13: 978-1-944737-09-2 / ISBN 10: 1-944737-09-X

1. Novel 2. Spiritism 3. Psychography
I. Lopes, Valéria II. Title III. Series.

CDU: 133.7   CDD: 133.9

Introduction

This tragedy took place in 1510, in a small village, in the South of France. It's said that love and hate are two emotions that walk hand in hand close to each other but never meet. This story is about the eruption of feelings when love and hate share one soul.

We are at the time of the Inquisition—a period when many atrocities were committed in the name of God. Out of sheer social prejudice, the matriarch of the Werck family forged a false accusation of witchcraft, with the intention of ending her oldest son's love for a beautiful peasant called Helen. Elizabeth had meticulously planned everything. Thus, to put into practice her sordid plan, before carrying out the false accusation to the Catholic Church, she sent her son Nestor to Paris on business.

The beautiful Helen was only 17 years old. As the accusation came from the Wercks, one of the most prestigious and richest families in France, the priests, representatives of the Catholic Church, and loyal to the wealthiest collaborators, all in the name of God, were not concerned about investigating the truth, so sentenced Helen to be burned at the stake.

During the trial the Inquisitor slandered, tortured and killed all of the defendant's closest family, in an attempt to confirm the monstrous lie that she was a witch. Afterwards, unable to force her family's confession, the allegation they clung to in condemning Helen to capital punishment was the simple fact that she had a black cat as a pet. This was the most convincing evidence they had and they used it against her.

However, these events unleashed extreme and supernatural reactions, when the immortal spirit of the accused became split between love and hate, with unforeseen consequences to the lives of those involved.

Chapter 1 - When It All Began

February 19, 1510

Dawn was breaking and the sky covered in black clouds announced the coming of a storm. The residents of a small village in Southern France had gathered at the square awaiting the day's big event. Some with great expectations and others with hearts filled with sadness. With her arms tied and her eyes blindfolded, there she was. Onlookers already knew her fate. Helen, the condemned, was going to be burned at the stake—serving as an example to the townsfolk as the expected and appropriate ending for those who worshipped a God other than the one embraced by the Catholic Church.

Elizabeth was there, too. In her eyes, was a slightly noticeable light of regret. Her initial intention had been different from what she now witnessed. She only wished for the separation of her son from Helen, not to have her killed. Elizabeth had never thought her plans would lead to the condemnation of Helen and the demise of Helen's entire family. But now it was too late for regrets. How could she explain the fraudulent evidence?

The only thing left to do was to pray and ask God for forgiveness, after all, she had not desired death for Helen. If she had committed a sin, it was in the name of a mother's love, so God would surely understand and forgive her. Unfortunately, Elizabeth had neglected one important act: to ask for Helen's forgiveness.

The inquisitor arrived at the square and ordered the torches to be lit and the execution to begin. When the fire was about to catch, Helen shouted:

"I'd like to make a request! I can, can't I?"

The executioner stopped and turned to the priest for the answer.

"Certainly," answered the priest, "and I sincerely hope in the name of God, that she will address those of us gathered here today in a proper tone of remorse for her sins."

Without wilting, nor any acknowledgement of the priest, Helen lifted her head and requested the removal of her blindfold. She wanted to die looking directly at the eyes of her persecutors, the people who were about to unjustly end her short life. With the priest's slight nod, the executioner stepped up onto the wooden floor toward Helen and removed her blindfold.

Helen's eyes revealed a strange darkening cold flame that was too much to gaze upon. She searched the crowd for eyes of pity but found none. The cold and inhumane attitude of the people on the square stoked Helen's anger. All there believed her guilty except for one priest, hunchbacked by age. For him, she was innocent. This was the priest from her village who knew her well. He attempted to help her escape sentencing, but was silenced and labeled unreliable, senile, by the inquisitors.

Helen couldn't understand the reason for this injustice. Not even the priest who knew her so well was able to save her from her fate, nor the hate that continued to rise up within her, adulterating her innocence. She had always worshipped God and had never committed any crime or act that went against the teachings of the Catholic religion. She always went to confession. Her biggest mistake was to love Nestor more than anything, including religion.

At one point, Helen's and Elizabeth's eyes met. Elizabeth tried to look away but couldn't as Helen's hate filled look cut deeply through Elizabeth's body and tore into her soul. Overwhelmed by regret, Elizabeth started to cry. Still, Helen's eyes did not move. At that moment, Helen shouted, quieting the crowd:

"I'll come back! I swear I will! I'll get my revenge on all of you. If I am a witch, as you claim, I'll find a way to come back and in the name of the Devil I'll succeed!"

The fire had started to go up her legs unleashing terrifying, sickening cries of pain from her writhing body. Meanwhile, her eyes, dark and otherworldly, blackened by hate, continued to stare at all, especially Elizabeth. Her last words, quiet and desperate words of love, that seemed most alien to the scene, were directed at Nestor who was not in the crowd:

"Nestor, I love you! Please arrive soon. I want to die looking into your eyes, into your love."

At the last moment clothed in fire, she called his name one last time—a whisper that hung stillborn upon the wind:

"Nestor…"

Never would anyone forget Helen's eyes. This terrible scene would be forever darkly etched in the minds of the witnesses. Suddenly, as if all in mass dropping to their knees, the townspeople collectively felt either guilt for not having helped her, or an animalistic joy at the sight of seeing someone being burned at the stake.

By now her suffering was ending. With sparks, smoke, and intense heat, that made the townspeople near the blaze gasp for air, all-consuming flames screamed towards heaven. Oddly, only one aspect of her was still visible, easily recognizable—Helen's eyes. They were still alive and wide open. Whether this was the work of God or the Devil nobody knew.

From a distance her body appeared as a brilliant bonfire beacon, as a horseman approached desperately shouting her name, asking God to arrive in time. He had heard in the Paris court from a friend about Helen's fate. With tears he beat his beloved horse, faster, faster while screaming:

"Helen, my love, wait for me! Helen!"

Nestor's despair was so severe that he didn't notice that it was too late. Breathlessly, he leaped from his horse and ran toward the fire, falling to his knees, struck down by the unholy trinity—sorrow, anger, and frustration—upon realizing that his efforts had been in vain. He looked up and caught a glimmer of Helen's eyes, dark, and wide opened, looking in his direction as if just waiting for his arrival before they would close forever.

In this way, Helen departed life creating an emptiness in Nestor's heart that he knew could never be filled. Some men mumbled, furtively glancing at the priests, how could they, the townspeople have allowed this tragedy to happen. For fear or indifference, they felt like criminals, and Helen's screams echoed in their ears with the words that one day she would return.

The storm finally broke forth causing everyone to run for refuge. With the rain, coiled in great gasps of smoke, the fire was extinguished and Nestor moved closer to Helen's smoldering corpse as he tried to gather whatever there was left of her. He moved slowly, dulled with pain and incredulity in what he had witnessed. He could not believe that so little remained of the woman he loved so much. Her being, body, was gone, as if she had never existed, except for her eyes that were still intact, unscathed.

Nestor took a step back. These eyes were not of his beloved—he did not recognize the dark light in them. He remembered her eyes as kind, sweet, and loving, never angry, never hateful. Elizabeth, who had witnessed everything, got closer to her son trying to console him as if she too were suffering. When she noticed the expression of terror in Nestor's face, she asked:

"What is it? Why are you like this?"

Pointing at Helen's eyes, he said, "Look! Helen's eyes did not burn!"

Elizabeth, terrified by such a ghastly sight, crossed herself and started to scream, causing people to turn and stare at her: "Can't you see? Come and look, she was really a witch! Only a witch could do that, come all and see this!"

At this precise moment, a long ragged lightning bolt reached down and ravaged the ground. The people overcome by fear, fled to their homes, chased by evil, branded by Helen's last words.

Elizabeth covered Nestor's eyes and pleaded with him: "Come on, let's go home, nothing more can be done."

Nestor grabbed his coat and used it to wrap around the remains of his love. Gently holding her ashes in his coat, against his chest, he said he would keep them. Since he could no longer have her, at least he would have her remains to be buried with him.

Nestor's words scared Elizabeth:

"You can't do that, it's a sin! No, Nestor, you won't take the ashes of this witch home! The priests won't allow it! Besides you will be accused of heresy and damned by the church."

"Mother, no one needs to know. With this rain, people can easily be led to believe that the ashes were washed away. But you need to be quiet now and stop yelling like an insane woman! It makes me think that you believed this absurd story of witchcraft. You're aware that this was all a lie, aren't you? You met her family and can attest to how religious and devoted they were. I just can't understand the reason for this injustice. What did anyone gain from it?"

Elizabeth ordered her son to stop talking. Each of his words cut into her anew like a sliver of glass, adding sharp pains to the dull mantel of guilt descending upon her. She wanted to forget everything.

"Please put these ashes anywhere but not in our house." At that, she walked away.

Elizabeth was soaking wet from the rain and feeling punished by the cold. This was not good for her health, since she was already of an advanced age. She left her son alone at the square and started to walk painfully, slowly away, trying to forget how guilty she felt seeing her son in such a sad state. So there stood Nestor at the square like a lost, bewildered child not knowing what to do—broken.

As she walked toward home, she thought of her son's suffering and realized that she had ripped away a piece of his heart. She also knew that Nestor would never forgive her if he discovered that she had caused Helen's death. This realization caused her to stop walking and bend over gasping for air. Nestor was her favorite child, the one that she had entrusted her family's future to, along with their immense fortune.

Besides Nestor, Elizabeth had three other children. Isabel, the oldest, had married well to the son of a French aristocrat and was about to give birth. Louiza, the youngest, was single and in nagging poor health. She had been born with a problem that caused chronic anemia, and as a result was constantly requiring medical assistance, which made her a very sensitive young woman. To compensate for her lack of health, Louiza possessed an admirable inner strength, which always shone through in her inspired charity towards others. Sebastian, the third child, was still young but pretended to be a man. He was arrogant, pretentious, and vain, living always under the impression that he could easily seduce any woman and have them fall at his feet in a heartbeat. One look cast in his direction and he believed the woman to be hopelessly in love with him. In truth, he was a fool. And then, there was Elizabeth's husband, Damastor— an old man with serious health problems that often kept him locked inside the warmth of the house. Louiza was Damastor's favorite child.

Isabel lived in the French court but had come to spend time with her family before returning to Paris where she intended to have her child. On that doomed afternoon, however, she wasn't feeling well and decided to stay home, preferring to stay with her father and siblings, instead of going to the town square with her mother to watch the execution take place.

As the rain started to fall heavily that afternoon, Isabel felt strong contractions and went into labor. At the exact same time, one of the kitchen staff in the back of the house began labor too. It was mayhem. The village's midwife had been advised about the helper's delivery and was already in the house to help with the birth. Louiza communicated with the midwife that there was another, unexpected delivery to be performed—Isabel's baby, who for some reason was struggling to arrive early.

Elizabeth had just entered the house when she noticed the movement of staff up and down the stairs. As she was taking her hat and coat off, she asked in a tired voice, one of the help who was hurrying down the stairs, the reason for all of the rushing about.

"It's your grandson, madam. He seems to be in a hurry to be born."

"That's not possible! The due date is not until April. It's too soon for him to come into the world."

As the words left her mouth, she felt the presence of someone next to her and felt her skin rising up in goose bumps. She stood still and breathed deeply, looking around her, but saw nothing. The servant noticed her madam's behavior and asked:

"What happened, madam? You look so pale!"

"Oh no, it's nothing, I'm just not feeling well because I suffered a lot in the rain. Go on and prepare something warm for me to drink and a footbath to soak my feet in."

At this moment, Louiza was hurrying toward the kitchen holding a stack of towels in her hands.

"Louiza! Why so many towels?" Her mother asked.

"Because both Dasdores and Isabel are giving birth. You should see the poor midwife; she is at a loss as to whom to help. She's upstairs right now with my sister and I'm trying to help Dasdores." Louiza left in a rush without saying another word.

When she arrived at the maid's quarters, a tiny room, she found Dasdores pushing, pushing and half of the baby's body was already out. The only thing Louiza did was to help pull the baby girl out. Louiza held her close in her arms and the child promptly started to cry. Louiza felt a rush of emotion. She approached the maid and lowered her arms so that the mother could see her daughter. She felt an odd touch of joy—elation that this child had chosen her house in which to be born.

Meanwhile, upstairs a weak cry led Elizabeth to the room where her grandson had too just been born. Isabel's delivery had been complicated. The midwife didn't know exactly why but warned the family that the baby was at risk and the mother might not be able to conceive again.

The midwife went on to explain to the family about Isabel's difficult delivery and the complications that could occur as a result. She also informed them about the delicate health situation of the newborn and the possibility that he might not survive.

"We don't have any means at our disposal here in the village and with this rain we can't call for the town doctor. The only option is to keep a close watch on the child for the next twenty-four hours. If he survives this period, a greater part of the risk will be behind us."

The midwife also recommended that the family seek the town doctor as soon as the rain allowed because Isabel's health had been so terribly affected. She excused herself to go to the cook's helper's room to check on the other baby. Upon arrival, she saw Louiza holding a baby girl and asked:

"What happened to Dasdores? She doesn't look well." And feeling discouraged she grumbled, "Why is everything going wrong today?"

"What do you mean? Dasdores is well!" Louiza said.

"No, Louiza! She is dead!"

Louiza was in disbelief and was only able to look at the bed where Dasdores lay.

"How can this be? She was talking to me just a minute ago and she was well. This can't be. Look again."

The old midwife got closer to Dasdores, held a mirror under her nose, and waited a little bit.

"I'm sure, Louiza, I don't know how to explain why, but she is dead. Everything that is happening today in this house seems to be the will of God because it's all like spears—swift sharp spears sowing discord, raining down upon this house."

Louiza was in shock at the situation she found herself in. With the child in her arms, she kept looking at the baby girl and at Dasdores without knowing what to say or to do. Louiza started to think about what she would say to her parents because they couldn't give the baby away to anyone; after all, she had helped to give birth to this baby and she felt responsible for her.

Meanwhile, her sister upstairs suffered from a high fever. Her newborn nephew was struggling to survive, but unfortunately could not draw breath for long and his heart was soon stilled. He had been born prematurely, too small with insufficient weight. As the midwife had said, it all looked like a divine plan.

Louiza was thinking about the midwife's words when she arrived at a plan of her own. She was going to speak with all of the members of the family, and if it was God's will, they would accept her proposal.

They were gathered in Isabel's room trying to console each other when Louiza entered, holding a beautiful, healthy, and glowing baby girl asleep in her arms. Her family was bewildered, but calmed by the soft, warm glow of Louiza's tranquility.

"Why is everyone crying?" Louiza said. "God took one baby away but brought another one: For me, it's quite clear he wants us to take care of this child as if she were Isabel's daughter."

All looked at her in expectation of what else was to come.

She continued, "My dear sister, Isabel, doesn't need to know any of this. We can alleviate her suffering. I can only think that since her health is already compromised, can you imagine what could happen if she finds out her son did not survive and that she will never be able to give birth to another child."

Louiza started to tear, "unfortunately, the mother of this child just passed away. Can you see how God worked all things out?"

Damastor, who always championed his favorite daughter's ideas, spoke first: "As always my daughter, you're right. I don't know what we would do without your calmness and common sense in times like this. But there's still something important to be settled. How will our son-in-law react when he finds out his son died due to our want of resources? We know that he feared for Isabel's safety with her pregnancy and opposed her traveling from the court at this delicate time. So, yes, the best we can do is to exchange the babies. Besides the four of us, no one else needs to know."

Sebastian added, "We will place the dead child with the deceased mother and tell everyone that they both passed away."

It was Elizabeth's turn to speak. She thought quickly and said, "How about the midwife? She saw the child and knows that Isabel had a son, not a girl. There's also Nestor. He won't agree to this."

Damastor replied, "The midwife should not be a problem. We can give her a good sum of money and send her to a distant place. As for Nestor, he doesn't need to know anything. We just have to keep the secret to ourselves. Isabel is unconscious and her husband is not here, so this makes it easier."

Louiza did not like, at all, the new direction things were taking. Her utmost desire was to help the orphan child who she now held in her arms, and the only way to do that, knowing how her family was and the prejudices they had, was to come up with this suggestion. She had given an idea about what to do with the baby, but her suggestion was taking on unexpected twists and proportions.

The family was now proposing to lie to Nestor, to Isabel, to her husband, and on top of that to buy out and send the midwife away. She didn't want to lie to Nestor, for she knew very well he would support her idea but disapprove of any lies.

Louiza said: "I think it's best if we think a little bit more about this. It's not wise to resolve things in such a manner—to lie. It's best to tell Nestor the truth and ask for his advice."

"No!" Elizabeth shouted.

"Nestor is in a bad state because of the death of that woman and in no condition to worry about his family at this moment. We must resolve this soon before the house staff learn the truth."

Everyone agreed with Elizabeth. So Louiza asked God to bless the child and her own good intentions, because she didn't want to cause pain, to hurt anyone. The family started to put the plan forth starting with the viewing for Dasdores and "her" son. All of the house staff attended, along with Louiza.

This tragic day, seemingly outlasting its own natural mortality, was not over yet. The torrential rain continued to fall paired with strong winds. Looking outside her window in the direction of the path that led to the house, Elizabeth waited for Nestor. During her wait, fear toyed with her—in the darkness of the night, a lightning bolt danced brightly and she could clearly descry two demonic eyes staring at her.

She let out a terrible scream and stepped back, away from the window while momentarily transfixed by the eyes looking in at her. It was late in the night and the entire family had already gone to their rooms.

Elizabeth's scream pierced the house. Family members hastened to Isabel's room from where the noise had come to see what was happening. At the doorway, they saw Elizabeth standing by the bed. She was looking at the baby resting next to Isabel, sleeping like an angel indifferent to the eyes of horror on her grandmother's face. At this moment, they asked in unison:

"My God, what was this scream?"

"Tell us Elizabeth, what happened? Why are you so frightened?" inquired Damastor.

Elizabeth turned and looked for a place to sit, trying to regain her breath, settle her heart. Unable to find any words about what she had seen, she replied:

"Oh, it was—it was just a nightmare. I think that I'm so nervous from today's events—I can't stop thinking about them. I don't know if you realize it, but today three people died, and two of them in our own house. Plus, Nestor is still not home, he is out there, in this storm that will not stop. I'm afraid, that's all. My heart is telling me that our lives are about to change. I look at this child and I get goose bumps. I'm exhausted, I don't even know what I am saying or feeling anymore."

"It's okay mother, go to you room, I'll stay here with Isabel," Louiza offered.

"Thank you, my daughter; I do really need to rest because I'm starting to see ghosts."

"Come on Elizabeth, don't be silly, you're just nervous," commented Damastor.

At this moment Nestor arrived at the house. Hearing the noises coming from Isabel's room, he knocked on the door and asked permission to enter. The family stopped talking and waited for him to open the door. Nestor was pale and his face was draped in profound suffering causing sadness to enter the room with him, infecting the entire family.

Louiza was the first to talk:

"Dear brother, I feel very sorry for today's events. I want you to know that I tried to help. I gave my testimony to the inquisitor about Helen and her family emphasizing that they were good Catholics. Unfortunately, my help was in vain."

Louiza hugged Nestor but noticed his stiffness, his emptiness—he seemed to be somewhere else.

For Nestor, it was like nobody was there, he was alone. He looked in the direction of Isabel's bed. Without realizing it, he started to walk toward the child next to his sister betraying no understanding, not knowing who the baby was. He held the baby girl in his arms and began to cry. He felt a strong emotion that could not be controlled and two tears came down his face. As if the baby understood everything, the child opened her eyes and played her part in the spirit of that moment.

Louiza became emotional too, as she witnessed this scene, understanding full well her brother's feelings. For someone who had just lost the love of his life, seeing a new baby, a new life, uncovered his heart, leaving it raw. In just a day he had witnessed the two most emotional events of life: death and birth. Elizabeth, wanting to see a quick end to all of this, took the child away from Nestor, laid her back on the bed, and guided a faltering Nestor to the living room.

Everyone followed them. They wanted to make sure that they heard Elizabeth's story to Nestor as to not fall into any contradictions when questions arose. After some explanations, Nestor, who was already feeling anxious to be alone, asked to be excused and headed for his room. Nothing he had heard at that moment held any importance to him. He did not have any sorrow left for the cook's helper and her child. He felt as if his heart had stopped beating while his body stubbornly continued to live.

Louiza, who was overcome by his depression, worried.

"We will need to have a lot of patience with Nestor. It will take a long time, if ever, before he forgets today's events. This period of mourning will be very difficult for him."

"Well, let's go to bed. Tomorrow there's much to do and each of you know how to proceed. I'll be in charge of the burial, and Elizabeth will talk to the midwife. Louiza will send a message and wait for the town's doctor; and Sebastian will send a message to Isabel's husband informing him that his daughter has been born and is doing very well," concluded Damastor.

What situations we create in our lives because we think we can resolve and choose the best path for the people whom we say we love, and through this excuse of love, we use all at our disposal, including lies, dissent and persuasion to manipulate life and influence death, playing God.

Unfortunately, the true feelings in this case were selfishness and prejudice pretending to be love. As always, there will be situations when the weakness of human beings will prevail and dictate actions. But the laws of the universe will come into play and all involved, in one form or another, will reap the fruits of their own acts and intentions.

Chapter 2 - The First Steps

February 19, 1511

As time often moves, unchecked, careening carelessly headlong sprinkled with forever moments, a year since Helen's execution went by in fits of starts and stops, and it was Leonora's first birthday. Guests gathered outside in the garden and children ran rampant creating an air of pandemonium on this fair weather afternoon. Sitting on a chair, Isabel shouted at Louiza who was busy trying to bring order to the joyful chaos as children sprinted around a table abundantly laded with sweet delicacies.

"Come on Louiza, bring Leonora with you, the priest is here and wants to see you."

Isabel gloated as she welcomed Father Samuel to the party: "She is a lovely child—you'll see Father—one cannot even tell that she was born prematurely."

The priest looked down trying to appear casual, and inquired about Elizabeth. He had not seen her in church for quite a while.

"She'll be down soon," Isabel said. "She is with my father upstairs, who, as you know, has been very sick and cannot do much anymore. In fact, nowadays she rarely leaves the house. My mother worries about his health and has no one to assist her since father will not accept any outside help—mother has to do everything. And as you can see, since I got stuck in this chair, all Louiza does is take care of me and my daughter. See Father Samuel, my husband hasn't been here in six months. So far, he has come here only once to hug and be with his daughter. He says that the climate here is better for both of us, but I know his mind. He simply does not want to take me, his ruined, handicapped wife to the Court. He'd rather hide me, hide these difficult facts. If I had borne a son he would have already scooped him away, but because I had a girl, he says that the best place for her is next to her mother."

"My brother Sebastian," Isabel continued updating the priest on the family news, "is carrying the family business since Nestor can't be counted upon. From that unspeakable, harrowing day Nestor hasn't been the same. He is quiet, wanders around the house, and goes out for long walks. Nobody knows where he goes. Sometimes he disappears for days, even weeks at a time. When he returns, his soul bears so much anguish that he locks himself in his bedroom so as not to see anyone. The only person who can still draw a smile from him is Leonora."

"You're saying he hasn't yet been able to erase, forget that witch? He's still suffering because of her?" the priest exclaimed with an authoritarian voice as if he were the God all mighty. "I better talk to this young man. I don't know why Elizabeth didn't share this with me because I would have taken the necessary steps to help a long time ago."

"What do you mean?" replied Isabel, "what would you have done?" Nestor will not listen to anyone, so why would he pay you any attention?"

"I would have already exorcised this ghost from his life. After all, don't forget that I was the inquisitor and therefore have the power to do so."

At this time, he was interrupted by a child pulling at his cassock. Leonora was looking intently into his eyes and the priest began to tremble even though she could not yet even produce any words. Like an earthquake, the trembling quickly spread and the priest's entire body shook, dominated by frightful deeply disturbing thoughts that emanated from just the sight of the child. Thankfully this powerful force was interrupted by a voice. It was Elizabeth's:

"Good afternoon Father Samuel, are you feeling well—have you met my granddaughter?"

Father Samuel fought to gain control over his fleeing mind. Elizabeth's grandchild: something about this child frightened him, awoke his instincts. Something was horribly wrong. He could feel it, but he could not identify the essence of his fear. Huffing with disgruntlement at his own weakness, he asked:

"Yes, I can see that this is a beautiful girl; but why does she bear little resemblance to the other members of the family?"

Standing nearby, Louiza overheard the conversation and promptly tried to subdue the priest's observation at such an inopportune hour.

"Come on, Father Samuel, she's still too little to resemble anyone; she is not able to even fully walk yet." To avoid any further response or challenges, Louiza took Leonora into her arms and moved away gingerly taking the child to play.

In the meantime, Isabel, who until now had not thought about the physical aspects of her daughter started to observe her to see if she noticed traces from the family line and thought: *Yes, the priest seems to be right; Her skin color is a lot darker than ours and her hair is so dark that it's almost black; Her eyes too, they resemble two black grapes, and her lips are surprisingly full; She has no traces from our family; Does she look like someone in my husband's family?"*

For the moment, she put an end to her newly sparked doubts about Leonora. One thing she was sure of—her daughter was beautiful, possibly the prettiest child in the neighborhood.

Elizabeth had walked away with the priest to talk in a more reclusive place and pretended that nothing had happened. She, too, had become quite disturbed by the observation made by the priest and the suspicion it created in Isabel. Elizabeth tried to manifest only a gentle calmness as they walked to allay the priest's suspicion.

"Let's go," said Elizabeth to the priest. "Let's talk in the living room where it is quieter. You know how loud a children's party can be!"

The priest was about to interrupt. But Elizabeth, feeling that he would continue with his questioning quickly asserted:

"You know, I was going to call upon you tomorrow. I'm glad you came here because I have been so tired—you saved me the journey. I go up and down these stairs several times a day. Damastor doesn't give me any rest; he rings for me, even for the littlest things, and refuses any help from the staff."

"Yes, Elizabeth, as you are quite aware, as a wife it is your duty to take care of your husband. Someday if, God forbid, you are ill, I am sure someone will take care of you. But tell me why were you planning to see me? You haven't told me that yet."

"Father Samuel, it will be a long conversation, do you enjoy the freedom of time to hold this conversation now?" He tried to hold back, to maintain his priestly gravity, but overcome by his curiosity about the path such a conversation might take, he replied quickly with a discreet smile:

"Of course, I'm always willing to hear my parishioners, to help them along the path of the Lord."

"Father, it's about Nestor. It was exactly one year ago that everything happened, or rather, started. After Helen's death, my son changed. He takes no interest in anything and spends his days wandering— no one knows where he goes."

"I know, Isabel has told me. Why didn't you look for me sooner?"

"There's more! On that fateful night, the night my granddaughter was born, one of the cooks died during labor along with her newborn son. My daughter for no tangible medical reason nearly died and became handicapped for life. And my poor husband, Damastor, now can barely get out of bed—he is so very weak and needs my help for everything. And for myself, you can see the results, look at my face, I don't know what sleep means anymore. Every night I'm afflicted with nightmares. I keep seeing those piercing black eyes, Helen's eyes, staring at me and accusing me of her death. I'm overwhelmed, possessed, tormented, by anguish and remorse for everything that happened."

Father Samuel interrupted her and spoke:

"What are you sorry for? You have no fault in it. She condemned herself by loving a different God, as such, partnering with the Devil. Do you want greater proof than what we witnessed that night? Have you forgotten that only her eyes didn't burn? That's witchcraft!"

"But father, I did nothing to help her. I knew she was quite religious and so was her family. I watched the tragedy unfold in silence. Let's not forget that it was me who denounced her. Now I question if I committed an injustice. Will there be any forgiveness for what I have done?"

"Come on, Elizabeth. Let's forget this. It's all in the past and there's nothing we can do now except pray for her soul to find peace. Pray and ask your son Nestor to come to see me. I'll try my best to be of help."

Damastor was shouting Elizabeth's name nonstop. All who heard his cries were frightened. Elizabeth and the father, who were in the living room, ran upstairs to Damastor's bedroom. Elizabeth ran in front, saying:

"Be calm darling, I'm on my way!"

"Come quickly, someone is trying to kill me!"

When Elizabeth entered the room she saw a black cat staring at Damastor. The cat did not move and his eyes did not stray from him. Damastor looked horrified.

"He came to kill me, take him away now!"

The priest grabbed a rag and shooed the cat out of the room while Elizabeth helped Damastor who had partly slid, fallen from his bed so half of his body was on the floor and the other half propped against the bed.

"Hush darling, all is well now; the cat won't come back."

With his heart further weakened by his reaction to the cat, Damastor struggled to speak. One could see his eyes and mind working, drowning in frustration as his tongue and lips failed to follow any direction. Finally, after minutes of intense anguish he said:

"Helen, Helen …"

Elizabeth turned white, looked at the priest, and both said in unison:

"What about Helen, tell us!"

But Damastor couldn't speak. Not at that moment and sadly never again, not for the rest of his life. On this night, Damastor became mute.

The following days only brought more suffering. Damastor's health worsened. He no longer ate or slept much, giving him the gray skin, and sunken face of someone who was already dead. He had lost so much weight that his bones seemed to poke at odd angles through his skin.

It was very sad to witness how a human being can suffer before death—especially for Elizabeth who remembered the fearless, handsome young man he had once been. Every night he shook, thrashed around in his bed in pain, and became agitated as if he were frightened at something. It was terrible what was happening to Damastor.

Elizabeth witnessed every long minute of Damastor suffering. She was exhausted and asked God to have pity upon his soul and take him away, to rest in peace. Only this way, Elizabeth thought, she would be able to go on. The children no longer came to visit him in his room. Seeing their father in such a state was far too painful for them to bear. Louiza prayed frequently for her father and asked God to forgive his sins, have pity, and take him to rest at his side so that he could be delivered from his pain.

The family, was greatly distressed by Damastor's condition—at night, they heard their father's low cries. The cries were like the sounds of a dog suffering, unable to find any other means to relate his tragedy. Leonora, standing up in her crib, would imitate the sound of her grandfather followed by what sounded like hearty laughter. Crowned in innocence, she would look around at the sadness of the family and start to laugh to gain their attention. The household was so downhearted by pain that it seemed the air, gaily scented air from nearby lavender fields, no longer entered through the windows—everyone, everything was suffocating in pain. Under these conditions, Sebastian asked his mother:

"Let's call for Father Samuel and have him bless this house. It is becoming unbearable to live here; there is something really bad around us. Can't you feel it?"

Nestor quickly accused Sebastian of being silly—the only reason everyone was so disquieted was because of the state of their father.

"There's nothing wrong with the house. Look how happy Leonora is; she in her youthful bliss cannot even sense our pathetic state. If there was something wrong in the house, wouldn't she be the first to feel it since no one has more sensitivity than a child?"

"Yes, it's possible, but I think Sebastian is right. We need to have the father bless the house and all of us as well," added Louiza.

Leonora, who was playing with a doll, paid attention to everything and often appeared to understand each word. Isabel looked away from Louiza and at her daughter for a moment and noticed that something strange was happening. Leonora really seemed to comprehend, and acknowledge the conversation, giving the impression that she was already an adult—not a one-year-old child. Isabel beckoned the others to note her observation, but at that moment Leonora resumed the beautiful and happy countenance of a child.

Elizabeth immediately called a staff member to send him to the church to look for the priest, to bade him to come promptly because her husband was dying. Thus the family decamped to Damastor's room to be by his bedside. Leonora was left behind, playing alone, while the family, all but Damastor, waited patiently for Father Samuel.

Damastor moved from side to side in bed sweating so profusely that his bed sheets had to be changed constantly. Isabel, plagued herself by illness, stayed near the window of the bedroom praying quietly, seeking peace—fear had overcome her. Very calmly, Nestor tried to help his father so he would not hurt himself while the others helped their mother to dry the spots on the bed that were wet. Their father's eyes and face remained in agony, fixated on one corner of the room as if something stood there.

Father Samuel walked in prepared to give Damastor his last rites. As soon as the priest started to pray, Damastor began to relax, the tension visibly flowing from his body. All the children had their heads down and asked God to hear their prayers. Leonora, meanwhile, had started to propel herself from her room to her grandfather's room. She crawled, half-walked and held on to the walls to avoid a fall. When she reached the room, she pushed the door open to enter.

She crawled in the direction of the priest and pulled his cassock. Startled, he looked down and saw Leonora with her small arms reaching upwards and talking:

"Grandfather, grandfather."

As the family heard Leonora's voice, they raised their heads and looked at her. "Grandfather" had been her first word. Nestor picked her up and brought her close to her grandfather who had his eyes closed, waiting for his hour of peace. Slowly she got near to his face, took his hair away from his ears and whispered.

No one was able to hear what Leonora said, but Damastor opened his eyes and turned to the window and saw a black cat. He gave a sigh, looked at his granddaughter, and died. For a few minutes, no one knew what to do. They were stunned by what they had just witnessed. Nestor was the first to react. He took Leonora from her grandfather's bed to her own bedroom. Every time Nestor had Leonora in his arms, she held tightly to him and didn't want to let go. It took superhuman strength to separate her arms from her uncle's neck.

"Ok, now you'll go to sleep, no more play, give me a goodnight kiss."

Leonora stared into his eyes and gave him a light kiss on the lips. Nestor was surprised. He felt confused and thought he was losing his mind. He left the room pensive and emotional about the kiss.

He couldn't understand the reason for his emotions, but at that moment, for a fraction of a minute, he felt a warm feeling in his lips like he had not felt in a long time. He rejoined his relatives who were taking care of the body and preparing it for the wake. No one spoke again about what had happened between Leonora and the grandfather. Everyone was quite somber at the wake, lost in their own sorrow or memories of Damastor, and naturally all was forgotten, but not by everyone. Father Samuel continued to be intrigued with the little girl and was waiting for the right moment to comment about the fact.

One month had now passed and Elizabeth had not yet fully recovered. She was still trying to regain the strength that she had lost from the previous year of suffering. Father Samuel blessed the house as required by the church and did not return again.

Since the day of the kiss, Nestor began to feel better—though he could not fully understand why. He walked around the house happier, smiled more, and had returned to work. Similarly, he could not stay away from Leonora. Every day, before his work, he went into her room and played with her. Everything appeared to be back to normal again.

Isabel's fortunes were also changing. She was happy. She had received a letter from her husband giving notice of his visit in three days. She felt so elated that she forgot that these days, following her father's death, required her to be in mourning. Instead she asked to have her most beautiful, pastel dress ready to wear for her husband. She was tired of being in black, in this bleak house and full of hope would ask her husband to take her with him back to civilization. She wanted Leonora to be educated in Paris and to frequent the court so she could have a bright future.

Isabel informed everyone of her husband's visit and started to make the necessary arrangements. The morning of his arrival she woke up earlier than usual. This was the big day, Rodolfo was arriving. She asked that Leonora wear a beautiful dress to wait for her father. Louiza affectionately brushed Leonora's hair, placed a lovely bow in it, and spoke:

"Now, darling, don't get dirty. Your father is coming and you want to look beautiful for him, don't you?"

"No! I want to look beautiful for Uncle Nestor," Leonora replied.

At this point, Leonora had already learned many words and everyone was proud of her phenomenal intelligence. She learned everything easily, was perceptive, and understood quickly what she was taught, especially when taught by Nestor. She paid attention to everything he said as if she were an adult. It was clear all around that the love she felt for

Nestor, was a love unlike any other. It was doubtful that such devotion would ever be captured by anyone else, not even her father.

The family was outside in the garden when Rodolfo's carriage pulled in raising the dust from the ground. Nestor and Sebastian hurried to welcome their brother-in-law at the main entrance. Isabel's husband was young and dashing with light skin and eyes the color of honey. A strong and healthy man, he was highly desired by the women from the court.

"How are you guys? It has been a long time! I received the note about your father's death and please accept my condolences. I wanted to come earlier, but because of my business I wasn't able to escape from my obligations until now."

"We are doing well, and you?" asked Sebastian.

"Very well, I miss my daughter. Where is she?"

Isabel freed Leonora from her lap and told her to go meet her father. Leonora started to walk toward Rodolfo but as she arrived closer to him she turned to Nestor asking to be picked up.

"No, sweetheart, here is your father, go to him as he misses you dearly."

Rodolfo held the little girl, hugged her tightly and walked in the direction of Isabel who couldn't contain herself. If she could she would have run toward him and thrown herself into his arms.

"Rodolfo, my love, I missed you!"

He kneeled and gave Isabel a hug. She offered her lips to be kissed but he pretended not to notice and started to speak:

"I can't stay long. I'm just passing through because I need to travel to start a new business out of France, probably in Italy."

Isabel flushed. She didn't know what to say because she felt surprised and afflicted by the news. Nestor interjected:

"Are you taking your wife and daughter with you?"

"Well, I'd like to talk about this later. Now I wish to spend a little bit more time with this beautiful girl I have in my arms."

The joyous atmosphere evaporated quickly. Everyone noticed that Rodolfo had just come to communicate his departure and had no real intention to take Isabel with him. Elizabeth, who until now had been silent, looked at Isabel and said:

"Don't worry, my daughter, your husband will naturally give us an explanation. Isn't that so Rodolfo?"

"Yes, of course, but right now I'm thirsty and exhausted. I need to rest a little from the trip. Let's go inside Isabel, later the two of us will talk."

The colorful visions that had ensued after Rodolfo's letter had now dissipated and only Leonora was smiling as she opened her presents.

"Look, Uncle Nestor, what a beautiful doll I got. Will you help me give her a name?"

"Of course my darling, later we will think of a lovely name for your doll."

A few hours had passed since Rodolfo's arrival—time enough to allow him to be feeling well rested. The family was gathered in expectation, waiting for him in the living room. Louiza had already put Leonora to sleep since the day had been quite eventful for the little girl with all of her gifts to open and play with. Isabel couldn't wait any longer and ordered one of the staff to go check if Rodolfo was up and to inform him that dinner was about to be served.

Twenty minutes later, Rodolfo entered the room looking rested and famished.

"Let's eat. Sorry for having caused you to wait for me."

He pushed Isabel's chair and affectionately placed hers next to his.

"You are looking beautiful and well-disposed Isabel, this climate really suits you. You are glowing!"

Isabel did not reply to her husband's remarks and instead showed him only a small smile. Everyone felt uncomfortable at the situation.

"Rodolfo, what kind of business are you planning to open in Italy?" Elizabeth asked.

"Well, I intend to continue with the same type of business I have now in coal and ore, but I also have other plans that I can't talk about now. After everything is resolved, I'll tell you."

"When do you plan to leave?" she continued.

"Tomorrow morning. I have a new business partner in Italy who is waiting for me, so I can't stay long."

Isabel looked at him in shock.

"Tomorrow? How? You won't take us? Why, Rodolfo?"

And Isabel started to cry. Elizabeth tried to console her but in vain. Then, she asked Louiza to take her sister to the bedroom. Rodolfo felt embarrassed but continued to talk.

"I can't take Isabel. What would I do with a handicapped wife and a child in Italy? I'll be busy with business and who would take care of them? After all, I'm going to another country where I hardly know anyone. First I'll adapt, learn the country and then make suitable arrangements. When all is well, I will come back for her."

This was the excuse Rodolfo offered. Nestor, infuriated by Rodolfo's coldness, got up and left. He knew his brother-in-law was lying. He had no intention to come back for his wife, at least if she remained unable to walk. As often the case, Sebastian's thoughts were far away from the family and he could care less about the present situation. So there was only Elizabeth left, who could do something:

"Do you know what you're doing to my daughter? She's crazy about you and your daughter is growing up without a father. Don't you have a heart?"

Rodolfo lowered his head in shame and replied:

"I'm very sorry. I didn't wish for any of this to happen but I haven't told you the whole truth. I'm in love with another woman. I'm going away with her but I didn't have the courage to tell Isabel. I feel pity for her. I'm young and I need a healthy woman who can bear children. Isabel can no longer do that. I need a son, that's the tradition. If I have no son, who will continue the family name? My last name can't disappear. I need an heir."

Elizabeth was shattered at what she heard. She came close to Rodolfo and whispered:

"Leave first thing tomorrow morning and never return. Have the dignity of at least continuing your lie to Isabel because as long as she believes that one day you might come back she will suffer less. Now get away from me."

When Elizabeth was leaving, she noticed Leonora sitting in a corner holding a doll and listening in to the conversation as if she could understand each word.

"What are you doing here, sweetheart? Shouldn't you be sleeping? Let's go, grandma will put you to bed."

Rodolfo was looking on, at his daughter, and asked:

"Elizabeth, who does Leonora look like? It's curious that her hair and eyes are so black…it's really strange, because I don't remember anyone with these characteristics in our families."

Rodolfo scratched his head and frowned waiting for an answer, which came quickly.

"If you were a real father to your daughter I'd give you an answer, but since you're not, you'll have to live without it," said Elizabeth.

Elizabeth turned around and walked away with Leonora. Later she shared with her children what

Rodolfo had said and reminded them to keep this news from Isabel, who was already terribly depressed.

Nestor and Louiza were devastated. They wept for their sister, knowing full well that she would suffer immensely if one day she learned the truth of his betrayal. Sebastian said that he had no trouble keeping a secret since he never cared much for his brother-in-law and none of it meant anything to him. His mother turned to him infuriated and spoke rudely:

"How selfish you are! You don't think of anyone else but yourself! I don't know whom you take after!"

"You don't mother? I take after you! Or do you think you're an exemplary person? You've always been cold with everyone except Nestor. Since he was different, you were caring and attentive. It has only been this one year that you've changed, and just a little. You don't notice everything I say or do because you only have eyes for your favorite son. But mother, I am your mirror. Can you not see your character within me?"

"Stop! Don't speak like that with our mother. Can't you see how tired she is from all of our recent strife? Have you forgotten that she has lost her husband?" Nestor shouted.

Sebastian got up and left, leaving Elizabeth to think about what had just happened.

"My son's right. I've always been selfish toward everyone except my family and husband. I never felt compassion toward people who came to me for help. I've always been as arrogant as Sebastian. I was frequently absent, simply lacking with my other children, except with Nestor; not to mention my biggest sin, bearing false witness. I hope one day God can forgive me and give me the strength to pay for all of my sins."

Life in the universe is constantly evolving, leading to our spiritual growth, where moments of pain are life lessons, opportunities to evaluate our choices and reflect on our weaknesses. Why me? What did I do wrong? Pain is a blessing in our lives, to help us know ourselves better and choose between awakening our consciousness or remaining in the illusion of the material world.

This awakening gives us the chance to seek answers for all of humankind's deep philosophical questions. Where do we come from? Where are we going? What are we doing with our lives? All of us will face these issues sooner or later, at least once in our existence. At such opportunity, we have the option to change our attitude towards life or to remain stagnant.

God in all his mercy perfectly weaved the net of events in their lives so that: Elizabeth would have the opportunity to learn about unconditional love through her granddaughter who was the reincarnation [1] of Helen, the woman who was condemned by the Inquisition and thus burned at the stake because of a false accusation of witchcraft forged by Elizabeth; Nestor would have the opportunity to reunite with Helen's love in the form of his niece, and in this way alleviate the pain of loss and fill the void in his heart giving him strength to continue to live; and Helen, who being reborn as Leonora, would have the opportunity to be next to the love of her life but at the same time next to and dependent upon the person she hated the most. Now as part of the Werck family, these two extreme emotions, love and hate would flare up intensely causing Leonora to struggle to choose between them. This would be her greatest challenge in this life.

---

[1] *Reincarnation* "the rebirth of the spirit after death, in a new physical body, for another period of learning and evolution." Allan Kardec, *The Spirits' Book* (Brazil: Federação Espírita Brasileira, 1996) 120, Chapter IV: The plurality of existences, question 166.

Chapter 3 - Hate Returns

February 19, 1520

The sun decided to shine brightly, to grace the Werck's family gathering to celebrate Leonora's tenth birthday. Leonora, like the sun, also shown brightly, sprinkling happiness on the family and guests as they relished the special occasion. Lighthearted joy pervaded everyone except for the one person who should be most happy for her daughter, Isabel. Since Rodolfo had left her, the exuberant happiness that had blossomed in Isabel's heart since childhood had been dried up and replaced with the darkness of anguish and revolt. Happiness was an emotion she no longer experienced. In constant lament for the last nine years, she had lost any taste for life—a story that could be easily read in her face. Sadly, over these years the lines of joy around her eyes and smile had slowly melted away to become lifeless, sunken shadows. She no longer had any desire to take care of herself, giving up the vanities in which women of her status and age commonly partook.

Today instead of celebrating, helping with party favors and games, she sat alone staring blankly at the ground. She often excluded herself from society, even shunning conversation with her closest relatives. If by chance she would raise her head to pay any notice to those around her, people would scurry away, for it was a signal that she was ready to begin, once again, to complain about her situation. Naturally her mother and siblings tried constantly to find and nurture even the smallest part of the old Isabel, the elegant, graceful, witty woman they loved, but this Isabel remained lost to all, drowned in melancholy. At times, Leonora felt pity for her mother and tried to distract her; but at other times, she looked at Isabel with noticeably spiteful eyes. Whenever Leonora acted this way, Isabel showed disbelief, disquiet that her daughter could look at her so. She told everyone about her daughter's strange stare, but no one paid much attention to her, nor believed her words.

Leonora, as delightfully commented on by her family, had the eyes of an angel, a soft voice and graceful gestures which were illuminated by the movement of her hands while talking. As a result, people suspected that Isabel's criticisms of Leonora could only be rooted in her own discontent. Isabel had even started to claim that Leonora wished for Isabel's death. All of the family responded to this startling assertion that it was nothing more than the result of a conversation that had occurred a few months ago— when Leonora, in a moment of anger, told Isabel that her father had left her because she was handicapped and ugly, and therefore had escaped with another woman, one who was beautiful and whom he loved deeply. At the time, Elizabeth ever protective of her eldest daughter said:

"Sweetheart, she's only a child, and doesn't know the gravity of her words so you have to forget them, she didn't mean to hurt you."

Through these periods of unrest between mother and daughter, despite their pity for Isabel, the Werck family defended Leonora whole-heartily. They claimed that she was a sweet, innocent child who was not aware of the impact of her words. In contrast, Isabel sometimes behaved like a crazy woman yelling in the middle of the night, calling for Louiza; but when Louiza arrived at her bedroom, Isabel could not answer any questions about her outburst, seemingly oblivious of her own behavior. Everyone began to accept the idea that Isabel's depression stemming from Rodolfo's heartless treatment had manifested into an irreparable psychological trauma.

Elizabeth loved her granddaughter. However, sometimes she didn't recognize her—especially when Leonora gaped at her and the traces on her face changed. It gave Elizabeth an uneasy feeling, like feeling watched by the unknown, unseeable, and she questioned her granddaughter each time this happened.

"What is it? You look very serious, is there something wrong? Tell grandma, why do you do this with your eyes?"

Leonora's response was always the same and consisted of a brief period of silence and a faint smile. But this was enough to put Elizabeth at ease.

Leonora, now ten years old, was a beautiful girl with well defined features that foretold the attractive woman she would become. Like many young people she used her innocence and beauty to her advantage and knew how to smile and catch the light with her eyes when asking for something so as not to be denied. Nestor, above all others, held her in special favor, having eyes only for her. He dedicated much of his time to her, gracing her with smiles, kind gestures, and encouragement. Even his solitary wanderings stopped as he now walked in the company of Leonora. On that special occasion of her birthday, he arrived with a large package. As soon as she spotted him, Leonora passed through the house running by her guests and threw herself at Nestor's arms kissing him all over the face.

"Have manners, Leonora," reprimanded Louiza. "You're becoming a young woman and should behave as such."

Her niece's extreme behavior toward Nestor was beginning to worry Louiza as unnatural, not proper.

"Come on Louiza, leave her alone. She loves her uncle and I love her too."

As Nestor was saying that, he gently unraveled Leonora's arms from his neck and gave her the gift he had brought. Leonora loved it. The size of the box only added to her curiosity, compelling her to tear it apart hurriedly.

"Take it easy," said her grandmother: "This way you will ruin the gift... so go slow, the gift will not run away."

Everyone laughed at Leonora's haste to open the present.

"She's really a child," thought Elizabeth.

She opened the big box just to find another smaller box inside and this continued for a while. After removing the wrapping paper of each box she found a smaller box inside. Leonora kept opening her present and looking at Nestor, however, not grasping what was happening.

"Keep going, there's more to be opened, you haven't finished yet."

She finally arrived at the last box and when she removed its lid her eyes sparkled at the beautiful jewelry box inside. It was a music box embellished with gold, small precious stones, and a little ballerina doll atop. This was the most delicate and stunning gift she had received, not to mention that it was the most expensive since it had been crafted by a renowned jeweler in Paris.

"Uncle Nestor, I love you…" Leonora said and pecked him on the cheek.

"So, you won't open the jewelry box?" he said.

"Of course I will."

When Leonora lifted the top of the music box another surprise! She found a gorgeous gold chain and a heart-shaped pendant. Even Elizabeth reacted in shock thinking that Nestor might have erred on his choice of a gift for a ten-year old.

"This present would be more appropriate for a candidate to be your future wife, don't you think my son? This time you went beyond the acceptable…" censured Elizabeth.

Leonora turned to her and with an evil eye made Elizabeth tremble. Elizabeth felt a rush of heat spread through her body, causing beads on her forehead, and nearly fainted. She was dumbfounded by the power of that look. It was time to share what she felt with someone else—this wasn't normal. It appeared that Leonora's eyes carried power that could only be from the depths of hell.

"What happened mother?" Louiza ran to assist her. "You almost fainted, are you all right?"

"Yes, I am fine." Elizabeth replied and turned to Leonora but at this moment her eyes had returned not only to their sweetest state but they also conveyed a feeling of deep concern and worry for her grandmother.

Watching this situation unfold from the beginning, a thought crossed Isabel's mind: *"There's something strange about Leonora. At times, it seems that she hates all of us, with the exception of Nestor, of course, but the majority of time she shows love. How can the sentiments of a child change so quickly? This transformation is so obvious—am I the only one who sees it? Mother must have felt something different about Leonora today and maybe that's why she almost fainted. Leonora almost knocked her out with her eyes. It's impossible that mother didn't notice anything!"*

Leonora, as if she were a mind reader, at this moment stared at Isabel and immediately Isabel looked away not knowing exactly why she felt fear, fear of her daughter.

The birthday party went on until midnight when the last guest left. Almost everyone at the house had already gone to their rooms except for Nestor, Louiza, and Leonora who remained in the living room.

"Uncle Nestor, tomorrow is Sunday, I'd love it if you took me out. It has been more than a month since we last went out together. What do you think?"

"My angel, I'd love to, but tomorrow, it is not possible. I have an appointment that I keep every year. Next weekend we will go out, okay?"

"But Uncle Nestor..."

Leonora started to scrunch her face to produce tears when Louiza interjected:

"Don't insist Leonora; your uncle has already told you that tomorrow is not possible; besides it's getting late—let's go to bed."

Leonora, looking very serious replied:

"I hope you don't want to take Nestor away from me as well." The threatening tone surprised both of them.

"Leonora, how can you talk to your aunt like this? Come and say that you're sorry."

"I will only say I'm sorry if she promises never to try to separate us, Nestor and me, from each other."

Louiza looked at Nestor. Leonora raised her voice and Louiza became scared.

"Never!" Leonora repeated.

"Leonora, I do not approve of the way you're talking to your aunt. Go to your room right now and don't leave it until I say so!"

This was the first time Nestor had addressed Leonora in this manner. She felt hurt and walked to her room with teary eyes. Not knowing what to say, Louiza looked inquisitively at Nestor—a spirit of apprehension gripped her tightly due to her niece's shocking changes of attitude and outsized display of affection for Nestor.

"Nestor, my brother, this little girl likes you in excess, so it's important that we are cautious with her feelings. She is too young and she may well be fantasizing, dreaming about you. Her demonstration of love toward you is worrisome."

"Don't worry, sister. Once she grows up a little, she will fall in love with a handsome young man and this sentiment for me will be a thing of the past."

"Yes, that might be true. Regardless, let's both be on guard about her behavior."

Even though these were the words that came out of Louiza's mouth, she had not convinced herself. In fact, she thought the situation was even worse than what it looked like. Leonora had a most noticeable, disturbing obsession with Nestor.

"Now tell me, where are you going tomorrow?"

Nestor turned serious and his eyes went blank as he looked away but answered:

"To the place I always go at the anniversary of Helen's death."

"That's true. Ten years have passed since then and you haven't forgotten it yet?"

"No! I dream about her almost every night. In this dream, I am running and running but I never arrive in time to save her! Wherever she is, I think she cannot nor will not ever forgive me."

Nestor cupped his hands to cover his face and started to cry.

"That day was horrible! That scene plays in my mind over and over again as if it had happened just yesterday. Her eyes so alive but full of pain and hate staring at me. My sister, I can't tell you how much I suffer. I am possessed and filled only by guilt as if I were the person who caused her to be burned at the stake. I used to love her desperately and I still do. I'm the only one who knows the pain I feel in my heart, every day, every moment, for this loss. Only the joy and presence of Leonora lessens my suffering, but sadly only a little bit."

"Nestor, you did all you could to arrive on time—it's not your fault. It's God who wanted it, made it this way." Then, Louiza got up, gave Nestor a big hug, and walked to her room to let her brother alone with his thoughts.

Dawn was breaking and Nestor had not yet slept. The previous night and the talk with Louiza had kept him awake. When one of the house staff arrived in the living room and saw Nestor, he said:

"Are you already awake Sir? Would you like to drink something before breakfast?"

"No, thank you. I will draw a bath and will be down soon for breakfast. I need to leave right after that."

Likewise, Leonora had not slept well. When she was going down the stairs, she met Nestor who was heading up and using a sweet, about-to-cry voice, she apologized to her uncle.

"That's okay Leonora, this time I will forgive you but don't do this again. Your aunt loves you and it's not fair to treat her in that manner, do you understand? And there's more: I want you to ask Louiza for forgiveness as soon as she is up."

"Okay uncle, I love you, please don't yell at me again. I couldn't sleep and it hurt a lot, did you know that?"

"Oh, really? Where did it hurt?" he replied jokingly.

Leonora slowly approached him acting like a victim and started to lower the straps of her dress to expose her heart and show him where it hurt.

"Here, right in the middle of my heart, can you see it? See how it's sad. Put your hand here and feel how it is beating."

At this she took Nestor's right hand and rested it on her heart.

"Can you feel how my heart reacts to the warmth of your hands?"

An electric current passed through Nestor's entire body and for a fraction of a second he forgot he was her uncle, and even worse, that she was a child. Nestor soon returned to the present moment and felt embarrassed not knowing what had just happened. He thought: *"How is it possible that this brat can make me feel desire? For a second, I saw her as a woman. I could swear she was trying to seduce me. How? Leonora, no, no, that's not possible, she is just a child who doesn't have the least notion of what she is doing."*

He tried to erase that thought from his head but when he saw her chest with little breasts exposed he froze and his heart accelerated.

"Stop!" he shouted. "You need to learn how to behave! You're not a child anymore; you are old enough to know better than to act this way!"

"Behave how, Uncle Nestor? What have I done to make you so angry with me?"

Her sweet manner left Nestor speechless and without strength to act with authority.

"All right, it was nothing. I need to go upstairs and take a bath so I can leave soon. You're still in your pajamas and the staff is already up, so go change too."

Leonora kissed him on the cheek and his face blushed from the warmth of her lips. This time he stifled his emotions. There was no place for thinking these thoughts, they are nonsense, he kept saying to himself.

Nestor had just finished breakfast when Leonora returned to the dining room.

"Are you going to be long, Uncle Nestor? I'd like to go out with you afterwards. Promise me that you will be back soon."

"It's okay, sweetheart, I won't be long. We will go out later." He gave her a kiss on the forehead and left.

Leonora gulped all of her milk and ran toward the window to see the direction her uncle was heading. She asked the staff to saddle her horse and thus rode behind, keeping a safe distance as she followed Nestor. Even if Leonora or a troop of horses were riding close to him, Nestor wouldn't notice it. He was lost in the thoughts and dreams of his past. He rode along paths on which Leonora had never ridden, taking shortcuts and venturing through dense bushes. He rode for almost an hour before stopping near some rocks.

Nestor got off his horse and walked through the spaces between the rocks. Leonora was hiding and watching his every move surprised that such a place existed in that region. She looked around and the arrangements of those rocks reminded her of an enchanted, magical place. She felt in the breeze about her, vibrations of a place that made her spirit leap, a place that she already knew, knew well, but couldn't recall having actually seen before.

"What is Uncle Nestor doing walking in between these rocks?" She was overwhelmed with mystery and her heart was beating at the excitement of this discovery. *"I wish he would leave soon."* Leonora started to rock back and forth in her saddle, impatient with the delay of her uncle. If she did not return home soon, family members would start wondering about her, asking questions. Despite all of her longing to stay and watch, to be with Uncle Nestor she had to go back. She vowed to herself that she would return to this place, the next day, to find out what mystery was hidden amongst these rocks.

Back at the house Elizabeth was asking about Leonora.

"That girl doesn't pay any attention to me, how can I know where she is? Naturally, she must be out with Nestor—let's ask the staff," said Isabel.

Louiza, who was coming down the stairs, hurried to answer her sister.

"She's not with Nestor. He told me he was going to leave early in the morning to go for one of his yearly outings. However, she might be riding her horse."

A second later, Leonora stormed into the house and started for the stairs, without realizing the women that were in the living room.

"Wait a second little girl, where do you think you're going?" asked her grandmother.

Leonora, as if in a hurry, kept walking and talking at the same time.

"I'm going to take a bath, because I'm dripping in sweat. I went out for a ride and it got a little late. It's so hot outside grandma, you should see it."

The mellow voice she used to address her grandmother melted Elizabeth, often rendering her defenseless. Anytime she did something wrong she used her sweet-sounding melodious manner. She was, indeed, a shrewd little girl who was well aware of the weak spots of each family member.

"You are not going to say good morning to your mother and aunt?"

"Of course I will."

Leonora walked toward them and gave them each a gentle kiss.

"Mother, how did you spend the night? You slept well, didn't you? I did not hear you cry out, as you so often do."

"Good morning aunt, forgive me for yesterday. I will never speak to you that way again."

Leonora gave her aunt another kiss using all of her seduction and sweetness. She eyed the three of them with a big smile and asked to be excused.

Later on the three women of the house were in the garden breathing in some fresh air, waiting for the time lunch would be served, when the dust in the air announced the arrival of a visitor. They waited until the rider approached a little closer, and identified the guest—Father Samuel. At the same moment, Leonora also arrived in the yard. Every time she saw Father Samuel her demeanor darkened. Isabel observed and took careful note of this transformation in her mind's eye.

"Good morning, ladies. Good morning, Leonora."

They replied in unison, and Elizabeth kissed his hand.

"Leonora, kiss father's hand and greet him like the good Catholic you are."

Leonora's eyes opened wide at her grandma's request, but there was no escape, she would have to kiss his hand. She grabbed the edges of his fingers and barely kissed it. For a moment, she had the urge to bite his finger, but she controlled herself. Her aversion to the father was clear to everyone around her, including Father Samuel who always felt strange in the presence of Leonora. Louiza, trying to disguise her niece's disapproving behavior, reprimanded her.

"Leonora, please don't act this way, what will Father Samuel think of you? Father, she's very sad. Yesterday, we had our first argument and so now she's behaving this way, please don't mind her."

Leonora who was very astute took advantage of this cue and added:

"That's right father. Please forgive me if I'm giving you a wrong impression about myself. It certainly wasn't meant on purpose."

Leonora started to walk away but kept looking at her aunt.

"Go to your room, I'll be there shortly," said Louiza.

"Excuse me," Leonora said.

Father Samuel watched Leonora walk away and commented, "I don't understand this little girl, sometimes she behaves in such a strange manner and her eyes appear to be filled with hate. You both will excuse me but it's time to take her to church. I haven't seen her there yet."

"Father, you are right, it's my fault," said Elizabeth. "Don't worry, next Sunday I'll bring her."

Taking advantage of this topic of conversation, Isabel added, "Your perceptions are well founded father. I've told everyone that Leonora acts in a strange manner but no one in this house wants to agree with me."

"Come on!" exclaimed Louiza. "She's just a spoiled child! I'm surprised, my sister, that you can have these thoughts about your own daughter."

"In all truth, sometimes I think she's not my daughter because she doesn't look like anyone in our family or her father's family. I also feel that she rejects me as a mother, as if we don't have the same blood running through our veins."

Elizabeth was starting to feel uncomfortable with the conversation, uncomfortable enough to promptly change the subject.

"Isabel, you don't know what you're talking about, that's why we don't pay you any greater attention. A mother would never talk like that about her own daughter," added Louiza.

"My dear daughters, please, let's change the subject," continued Elizabeth. "I believe the reason for

Father Samuel's visit was not Leonora. Would you like to join us for lunch, father?"

"No, but thank-you Lady Werck, my visit is brief and I just wanted to ask about the absence of Leonora at the church. I feel more at ease knowing that I will see her there next Sunday. Isabel, you too, please come. The sermon and prayers during mass will make you feel better, after all, you'll be in God's house."

Louiza didn't want to hear any more comments about Leonora from her mother or Isabel, so she discreetly stepped away. This situation did not sit well with her. She loved Leonora as if she were her own daughter but she also could not deny that her mother and sister had reasons to think that there was something strange about her niece. After all, thought Louiza:

"Leonora was only a ten-year old child. How was it possible for her in certain situations to act as a grown woman? When this happened, her features would change, her eyes would enlarge and appear to emit fire, her voice would transform, everything about her would appear differently. Then, in a split second she could turn back into the ten-year-old that she was—a beautiful little girl affectionate and lovely. This behavior was indeed bizarre. Father is right, maybe it's best that she starts to attend service."

Louiza entered Leonora's room and found her lying on a bed embracing a cat.

"Where did this cat come from?" asked Louiza surprised.

"He's mine aunt Louiza. I've had him for a long time, but please don't tell grandma, okay?"

"How do you keep this cat and yet no one has ever seen it?"

"It's because I always hide him whenever someone approaches. I know everyone in this house is afraid of him since grandfather's death."

"What do you mean Leonora? What are you saying?"

Frightened by this conversation, Louiza started to wonder: *"How can she remember this story? She was too little for that and if my memory doesn't fail me no one in this house ever touched this subject again."*

"Leonora, tell me! How do you know the story about the cat and grandpa?"

"I remember, Aunt Louiza. I remember everything even what I whispered in grandpa's ears right before he died. I said, Grandpa die soon or I'll open that window and let the cat come in and lap up your soul."

Shocked, Louiza didn't want to believe what she had just heard. She became pale and sat on the edge of the bed holding the covers tightly so as not to fall.

"Listen to me, don't tell this to anyone... anyone."

For the first time in her interactions with her niece, Louiza truly quivered.

Downstairs lunch was coming to an end and Elizabeth noticed that Louiza had barely touched her food. Full of worry because she had never seen her daughter like this, she said, "Are you sick, my daughter? It looks like you are not feeling well."

"Don't worry, I just feel a bit queasy, it will pass soon."

At this time, Leonora stood up from the table. She was anxious. In fact, several times during lunch, she had got up to look outside the window.

"What happened Leonora? Why are you nervous? Did something happen?"

"I'm worried about Uncle Nestor. He left early this morning and promised to return soon to take me out."

"Don't fret. When he goes on these rides he takes a long time and sometimes he even does not return on the same day."

"No! He promised to return early! He won't forget about me. I'm sure of that!" Leonora shouted.

Leonora was hysterical. The simple mention that Nestor might have forgotten about her was enough to alter her expressions and when she spoke next she was once again speaking not as a ten-year-old but seemingly as an adult woman.

"He never forgets what he promises me!"

"Now, you think your uncle has nothing else to do but to flatter you!" said Isabel.

Isabel's tone of voice was harsh as if she really wished to bruise her daughter with words. At this moment, Leonora leaped from her chair toward her mother. She did it in such a way that everyone on the table froze and stared with disbelief. It looked like Leonora were going to hit Isabel to quiet her.

"Shut up right now! You only speak nonsense! Go look at yourself in the mirror, you look ridiculous! Do you think everyone is like you! Be careful Isabel, you are already unable to stand or walk, do you want to be mute too?"

Leonora's menacing tone shocked her mother and aunt into speechlessness. They couldn't believe what they were seeing or hearing. The change in her voice was unordinary, supernatural. Leonora continued:

"Never, ever, not anybody, not even you, will take Nestor away from me. Your presence is only irksome, never pleasant, but I'm sure that because your own love is but a wilted flower, you simply cannot understand, nor accept my love for Nestor, a love you haughtily deem improper. As if you are fit to judge me! So my only words to you are, be careful, very careful my dear mother!"

At the end of these words, Leonora turned her back, opened the door and went to the garden. Her arrogance transgressed, subdued all lines of propriety. Elizabeth was in shock and for a few seconds she could swear she had seen in Leonora, Helen's eyes. Louiza, who was still disturbed from the earlier conversation with Leonora in the bedroom, once again entered a state of numb disbelief with what she had just witnessed. She tried to get up to help Isabel who was stupefied, but her body didn't want to move. In this exact moment, Sebastian arrived to help them.

"What in the world is happening here? I just passed Leonora in the garden who was crying nonstop and unable to utter a word. I entered the house and see all of you in this pitiful state as if you had all just seen a ghost."

No one replied. Elizabeth struggled to get up and leaning against the walls made her way to the bedroom. Sebastian stood there not knowing what to do and waited for an explanation from her sisters. Louiza, also silent, grabbed Isabel's wheelchair and they too went to their bedrooms.

Sebastian shouted, "I do not understand anything, what happened!" No one answered him. He shrugged and said, "Whatever! You don't want to talk... don't talk!"

Sebastian collared a lingering staff member, whom he inquired about Nestor, and whom he asked to prepare something to eat. He awaited there for his brother. The sun was already setting when Nestor walked in. As he entered the house, he found the environment to be of a deep, pervasive silence, which was most strange for that time of the day.

"Saturday afternoon and nobody is home!" shouted Nestor as he walked in the door.

Sebastian, who was standing a few feet away, replied, "Actually, everyone is home but they have already retired to their rooms. I'm here only because I'm waiting for you. When I arrived today I was met with perplexed, puzzled faces. Every woman in this household appeared stunned."

"Did you ask what had happened?"

"I asked but nobody answered," said Sebastian.

"I don't have the least idea either because when I left early this morning everyone was still asleep," added Nestor.

"Nestor, something very serious has happened. I have never seen our mother and Louiza in such a state. Their expressions were strange—I even asked if they had seen a ghost."

"Well, we'll find out. I need a bath first and then I will ask Louiza. By the way, why are you home? It's rare to see you at this time of day. Did something happen to you as well?"

"No, it's just that I had a date with a woman but she didn't show up. Can you believe that? That has never happened to me before."

Nestor worked up a sympathetic smile. "It's part of life, my brother, rejection sometimes happens. You're getting older and shouldn't think that you can keep your youthful looks forever and act with abandon as you have done so far in life. Things change as one ages, you'll notice."

Sebastian listened attentively to his older brother's words of wisdom. This was true, he reflected, like Nestor, he had passed the marrying age and until now had not found the right woman with whom to start a family. Truth be told, in the Werck household, except for Isabel, everyone was past the marrying age.

"I'm on my way up, and will talk with you later," said Nestor.

Louiza was lying in bed resting when she heard a knock at her door.

"Come in please," she beckoned.

Nestor stepped in and did not engage in trivial conversation but pushed straight to the question at hand. "Tell me what happened today."

"My brother, I'm not sure how to tell you this, but it's about Leonora."

"Leonora? What about her?"

"Keep calm, I'll tell you. I don't know if I'll be able to explain exactly how everything happened because I have never seen anything like it."

"Hurry up, Louiza! The suspense is troubling me."

Louiza proceeded to recount the events of the day in great detail while Nestor listened without blinking.

"And Isabel, how is she?" Nestor asked with concern.

"She's in her room now and is in a regrettable state. She is refusing to talk. As for Leonora, she too is in her room crying without end about her behavior. Mother is shaken. We don't know what to do. The only thing I know for sure is that Leonora needs to be helped and Father Samuel might be the person who could help us."

"I don't know about that," said Nestor in disagreement. "You know that I don't like him. He's an inquisitor priest and responsible for taking away from me the only woman I've ever loved. I'll talk to Leonora, and then we can decide what to do."

After Nestor left Louiza's room he went to talk to Leonora. He knocked at her bedroom door three times but nobody answered so he slowly opened the door. Leonora was sleeping. Her face was like an angel with an expression so soft as if she were in the hands of God. As he took in this scene, it was hard to believe any of what he had heard. As he approached her bed, a feeling of love and agony overcame him. He wanted to hold her, put her on his lap, protect her, and gently smooth her hair. At this moment, as if feeling his presence, she opened her eyes and spoke softly. "Sit here, Nestor, next to me, I need you so much."

That's exactly what Nestor did and Leonora nestled her head in his lap as she began to faintly sob. He couldn't resist her charm; he wanted to speak but was at a loss for words, he was utterly infatuated with her. He smoothed her shiny, soft hair, and with closed eyes got lost in the emotion of the moment, experiencing great tranquility in his soul. She gave him all that he needed, which was a sense of peace. Leonora knew this, and at intervals she would look up to check to see if she were achieving her goal. She succeeded as Nestor did not talk with her about what had happened that day.

And once again, she thought: *"I won one more time! If they think they can keep me away from Nestor they are dead wrong. I'm capable of doing anything to keep him close to me."*

The next morning came quickly and everyone was up early. Breakfast was served, but before, during, and after not one word was exchanged. No one knew what to say until Leonora broke the silence and acting as if nothing had happened spoke in a kind manner using a tone of regret.

"I want to apologize to all of you for what I said yesterday. It was not my intention to say hurtful words, but please understand me mother, emotion overcame me. Grandma, believe me, I love all of you. I'm very grateful, especially to aunt Louiza who is like a second mother to me. Sometimes, I don't know what comes over me, but I promise it won't happen again."

Her eyes begging for forgiveness moved Louiza and her grandmother, but did not convince Isabel who at this point nearly despised her own daughter. Leonora looked into her mother's eyes and read them like lines in a book, but faked ignorance. She approached her mother, kissed her on the cheek, and asked for forgiveness. In that moment, Leonora seemed to be telling the truth, and even Isabel felt it as sincere regret from her daughter.

"Okay, let's forget everything," said Nestor as he got up, kissed his mother, and started to make his way out of the room when he was stopped by Leonora's request.

"How about my kiss, will I not get one?"

"Of course you will, your jealous little girl!"

Nestor kissed her and left the room.

Leonora's face lit with victory. She looked at all the women at the table with an expression of satisfaction conveying in a few words that Nestor did everything that she asked him to do.

"I'll go for a walk now to think about my mistakes. I promise you that I'll pray too. Grandma, you will see how I am capable of changing, I swear I will change!" Leonora concluded triumphantly.

"That's nonsense," said Elizabeth. "I love you and you are a gentle and sweet girl—keep being this way. Don't let hate overtake your heart. The sentiment called hate was not made for you and will not bring you anything good; this is the only thing you have to change. Well, go take a walk, the early morning sunlight and the fresh air will be great for you. Why don't you take this opportunity to stop by the church to pray? You will feel better, my angel."

"Yes grandma, I'll do that," Leonora replied.

She kissed everyone one more time and left. She asked a stable worker to saddle her horse and then took the same path as when she followed Nestor to his hiding place. As she started off on her exploration, Leonora felt the thrill of childhood! Even though she was a child, she did not always act as one. She felt lighter and freer than she had in a long time. As she rode, her thoughts were of Nestor stroking her hair, looking at her with loving eyes, all of that moments were to her like a balm, for it brought peace to her soul.

Leonora couldn't understand the shift that happened inside of her from love to hate when someone threatened her relationship with her uncle. The only person who she had never felt hate for was Sebastian due to his aloofness and lack of desire to get involved in family matters and her love for Nestor. She loved her mother, her aunt and especially her grandmother, however, her hate always seemed to escalate toward Elizabeth. This caused Leonora some confusion. How could she love and hate at the same time? Lost in thoughts and trying to make sense of her emotions, she was brought back to the present by the sight of the same place with rocks, that she had seen the day she had spied on Nestor.

At this moment, her heart accelerated and all of a sudden she became anxious and confused. As she got closer to the entrance, she felt an unexplainable tightness in her chest, but being the stubborn girl that she was the only option was to keep going and find out what this place meant to Nestor. What did he do here? Why did this place entice him to return year after year?

She got down from her horse and started to walk through the tiny passage, barely wide enough for an adult, through the rocks. She was nervous and hesitant, and even felt a chill in her spine, but regardless of these feelings she kept walking forward. She kept moving straight ahead and at the end of a narrow passageway there was a grotto with a small entrance, so small in fact that Leonora had to bend over to go through it. Standing by the entrance, she stopped and looked around for a few seconds and thought: *"I'll go in. If this is the place Nestor comes, I want to know what is so important about it."*

She put her head in first and tried to look around, to spot anything out of the ordinary. Unfortunately, the place was quite dark and she had to advance inside a little in order to have a more complete view of the chamber. Once she was in, she straightened herself up and looked around until she was able to adjust her vision and see better through the darkness and to the back of the grotto.

A small flash of light illuminated some sort of altar or a stone table, it was hard to tell. She looked from one side, to another, and concluded that was it. There was nothing else in the grotto. Leonora felt disappointed with her discovery because there wasn't anything more interesting to be seen. She walked forward to get closer to the table to examine it, to make sure that there wasn't anything else there. She felt so frustrated that she nearly started to cry from disappointment, and thought: *"I can't understand what Nestor does here."*

Once again, Leonora looked around and then passed her hand over the table to check if it were real. She did that for a few seconds until a chill ran through her body. She had a feeling that there was somebody else with her.

She looked around quickly but saw nothing, just emptiness. However, her instinct told her that someone was staring in her direction. Her first instinct was to run, but her legs did not obey. She was scared, she wanted to shout, but her voice had become hoarse. She could barely hear herself, until she mustered some strength and with great effort asked a question:

"Who's there? Is there anybody here?"

Suddenly she spotted someone but had to rub her eyes to make sure that there was in fact a person there. Yes, an old man not wearing a shirt and a little hunchbacked sat next to the table. Not believing the image was real she kept opening and closing her eyes, until her doubt faded away.

"He's real," she finally confirmed to herself.

He was there, looking away from her, and the strangest part of this was that her fear and dread dissipated immediately. She started to walk toward him when a voice came through the grotto.

"Stop, that's enough. Don't come any closer."

"Who are you?" Leonora inquired.

"Can't you recognize me, Leonora? We are old friends. I've been waiting for you for a long time," the old man spoke.

"How do you know my name? Do you know me? I don't remember having met you."

"Well, Leonora, I've known you for many and many years. I've been in this grotto waiting for you to become a young lady, only then would I be able to help you. All of these years before, I have taken care of your old soul or what is left of it."

"I do not understand what you're saying. Did Uncle Nestor tell you about me?"

"Oh no!" he grinned. "Your uncle doesn't know me but thanks to him I ended up in this place."

"Well, now I really don't understand what you're saying. Please be clearer, but before we proceed can I please know your name?"

"My name is Bartholomew, for now that's all I can say. You'll have to be patient and with time I'll be able to better explain everything you need to know. You're still too young to understand, but I want you to know that I'm like a guardian angel. Do you know what a guardian angel is?"

"I think so," Leonora replied feeling better and more at ease. "My aunt has read many stories for me where they talk about how children have guardian angels. I didn't think it was true. Does that mean that in all that I ask of you, I will have your help?"

"No, it's not quite like that. I'll be able to help you by giving advice and trying to make you recall a distant time in the past that still lives inside of you. I'll need to teach you how to forgive and after that I can take you back with me."

"Where do you want to take me? I will not go with you anywhere, do you hear me?" Leonora started to become aggravated with what the old man had said, not the part of him wanting to take her somewhere, but the thought that she would be leaving Nestor behind. She then added: "I'll only go with you if you take Uncle Nestor as well."

Bartholomew gave a small smile, looked at her with great patience and kindness, and said, "You don't need to act like such, for I will not take you away until you ask me. You will only go with me when you want to, when you are ready. Right now, we are just talking, nothing more."

"Okay, guardian angel, we are at a better understanding with each other now. Can I call you guardian angel?"

"Yes, you can, but from now on you need to start praying. You are in need of a lot of prayer because your soul can't find peace."

"When I hear the word soul, I don't understand it. What does it mean?"

"The soul, my child, is who we are, and this physical body that we have covering us is simply matter. What is really true is what is found deep inside, hidden in you and in your heart. This is what we call soul, our true essence, and that never ends. Your physical body decays when you die, or sometimes, decays even in life, but your soul lives forever, it is eternal."

Leonora reflected for a few minutes on those words and then asked, "so my soul is not at peace and for this reason I need to pray for it? But tell me, why isn't my soul at peace? What disturbs it so much that she becomes like this, suffering, and in need of a lot of prayer?"

"It's the feeling of hate, my child, it is your spirit's ignorance of not knowing how to forgive, but this you will only understand with time. At this moment, what you need to learn is to have faith, to believe in God, learn how to talk with him, and rid your heart of all this pervasive hate. Only then will your comprehension of life improve and your questions become answered."

"So, you're saying I have to go to church as my grandmother has asked me to, and listen to that priest whom I can't stand?"

"Yes, and I'll be able to teach you as well, but you will have to go to church. This will be the first step toward forgiveness and to learn of God's love."

Leonora felt disturbed by the words of her guardian angel, she didn't know why, but as she heard about God's love, she felt some fear.

"Now it's time to go home, it's getting late," Bartholomew told her. "Anytime you need a kind word, just come here and you will find me. I will be waiting for you. Never forget that."

After saying that, Bartholomew faded in the air leaving Leonora amazed and at the same time intrigued by the spiritual experience she had lived. A few minutes later, after calming herself from all of the emotion she had felt, Leonora began to remember every little thing that had happened, was convinced that everything was real, and thought: *Unbelievable! I saw and talked with my guardian angel...*" Still wrapped in her thoughts, she decided to follow the advice from Bartholomew and her grandmother. Without hesitation, Leonora mounted her horse and headed toward the village with the intention of going to the church to pray.

This was Leonora's first contact with the spiritual world. She didn't know yet about anything that was happening, but with time she would come to understand the significance of this event, and how much this spirit helped and would help her during her life, and the necessity of this meeting as it was. Thanks to her curiosity, this moment had happened.

As she rode by the church, she stared at it from a distance and just couldn't imagine herself inside—but a desire so strong overcame her that she began moving toward it. The last time she had sat in the church was when she was very little and she could now not remember anything about its interior. Through the stories that Elizabeth had told her, she had learned that she used to cry a lot in church, disturbing the priest to the point that she had to be taken outside so he could proceed with the service.

Standing outside the church, Leonora looked closely at each of the windows until she noticed that one of them was ajar. This window was just a bit out of her reach, so she hunted for a rock or piece of wood to stand on. She found a piece of wood nearby, placed it underneath the window and in a slow manner as not to be noticed by anyone she managed to extend the window open.

Then, Leonora peered inside. There were women praying in a whisper, men lighting candles, and the inquisitor priest with his austere voice speaking nonstop. She felt a chill upon hearing his voice. She just couldn't tolerate it. She felt fear and hate, and became possessed by terrible thoughts. For a little while she kept staring at his embroidered clothes until something darkened her vision.

Leonora felt a strange sensation, as if her body was catching on fire. A strong heat was going up her legs, she wanted to shout for help, but all of a sudden, like a lightning bolt, an image appeared in her mind. It was fire, a ball of fire. Without realizing it, she was looking fixedly to a candle that was near the priest and with a strange, supernatural feeling of hate at play in her eyes she wished for his clothes to catch on fire.

The priest sensed an evil energy in the church and looked in the direction of the window where Leonora was standing. He saw her black eyes spitting hate, like the stare of the devil. He felt terror. He looked down and his clothes were on fire. Everyone in the church started to scream, except for the priest who was still and unmoving, seemingly caught in a trance, hypnotized. The people ran toward him trying to put out the fire that had climbed rapidly spreading all over his clothes, his body.

"Priest, for the love of God, wake up! You are in flames!"

A woman shouted desperately at him, to wake up, to jar him out of his catatonic state. Leonora, amidst all the confusion, returned to her normal innocent self, and became very frightened about what she had just witnessed. She stepped down from the wood block and quickly left the disturbing scene behind her. She rode her horse fast towards home. She felt horrified of her power because she remembered clearly having the horrible thought and then seeing it materialize in the burning clothes of the priest.

When she arrived home, she sprinted to her room. Immediately, she opened her wardrobe looking for her cat but couldn't find him. She called him quietly until he appeared at the window. She opened the window and let him in. She held him, stroking his coat and telling him in confidence about what had happened.

"You know what I did, don't you?" she asked him.

She stared at him as if he were giving her an answer.

"Well, I think the priest is severely burned."

A small smile came over her face.

"The worst part is that I think he saw me, she continued, so he will come here and gossip to grandma. I'm afraid, I need your help, I don't know what to do. He can't talk about what happened with anyone."

As if the cat understood every word she spoke, he licked her face and left in the direction of what might be his next prey.

The rest of the week passed well. Leonora kept attentive, to listen, to hear if anyone should come to the door, always afraid that it might be the priest. When she was sure it wasn't him, only then could she breathe a sigh of relief. Isabel, who never took her eyes off her daughter, noticed that something strange was happening, but she kept to herself. In fact, she refused to talk to or about Leonora. She'd rather just silently observe her.

After that terrible episode with Leonora, Isabel's health had worsened tremendously. She was very weak, coughed a lot and breathed with great difficulty. She barely left her room, and did not speak with her relatives. She was spending her days in a trance as if she were already absent from the world.

Sunday morning had finally arrived. Elizabeth woke up early and asked Louiza to get Leonora and Isabel up as well so they could leave together for the church, as she had promised Father Samuel. First, Louiza talked to Isabel who surprisingly was already up and ready for breakfast; next she knocked at her niece's bedroom door to let her know about the church outing with her grandmother. As the word "church" sank in, Leonora blushed and immediately started thinking about what to say or do to get out of this commitment. Immediately, she decided to fake an illness and with mastery forced out a series of coughs and acted out with words and gestures a severe headache. She played the role of sick child as well as any professional actress.

She performed this act so well that Louiza went straight to the living room to inform Elizabeth that Leonora wasn't feeling well. This raised great concern within the household because Leonora had never fallen ill—having always displayed excellent health. Nestor became visibly worried and visited his niece's room frequently to check to see if a fever had developed. The only one who was not fooled by Leonora's story was her own mother, who for one reason or another knew that Leonora was lying. *"They are all idiots,"* Isabel thought, *"this girl makes everyone look stupid. One day they will find out her true self, forgive me God, but she is not my daughter, I feel that."*

Isabel started to cry and Elizabeth spoke:

"Please don't be sad. She will get better—you don't need to cry."

Isabel raised her eyes to make eye contact with her mother, and for the first time following the announcement of Leonora's feigned illness, she spoke:

"Mother, let's go to the church—I need to pray."

Isabel knowing that her skepticism, suspicions of Leonora would be met with disbelief kept her thoughts to herself.

"You're right", said Elizabeth, "Let's go. Father Samuel deserves at least an explanation. I don't want him to think that I forgot my promise to take Leonora to church."

Elizabeth asked Sebastian to get the carriage ready, a request he met with unusual promptness and without complaint. Elizabeth was quite taken aback by his thoughtfulness and attitude about attending church. *"He didn't say anything, didn't even complain, how strange! Something is wrong with Sebastian."*

She was unaware that Sebastian's changed demeanor was a matter of the heart. He was in love with a Catholic girl who rarely left church. Wanting to see this girl, there was nobody who desired more to go to church than he did. As they came to a stop at the front steps of the church, Elizabeth began to help Sebastian carry Isabel out of the carriage.

A priest welcomed them: "Good morning, how are all of you doing? I'm very happy to see so many of the Werck family members here, and how about our Leonora?"

"We are fine, thank you," replied Elizabeth. "As for Leonora, she caught a cold and had to stay home. Louiza and Nestor are there taking care of her."

"Well, please come in, the mass is about to start," said the father in a rushed manner.

"Isn't the inquisitor father conducting the service today?"

"No, madam," answered the substitute father. "You don't know what happened to Father Samuel?"

"No," replied Elizabeth and Isabel at the same time. "What happened to him?"

"It was quite tragic, but now I have to start the mass—please meet me at the sacristy afterward and I will tell you in detail about poor Father Samuel."

Isabel felt her heart tightened as if she knew Leonora was responsible for the fate of the priest. She couldn't articulate reasons for her thoughts, but she had a bad presentiment about this, or better, a prophecy.

Curiosity took over, and both Elizabeth and Isabel barely paid any attention to the mass. They were worried and anxious to learn the details of Father Samuel's tragedy. As soon as mass was over, they made their way to the sacristy leaving Sebastian alone in the church—as he allegedly wanted to stay there a bit longer for prayer. For the second time in the same day, Elizabeth was surprised with Sebastian's attitude but now was not a good time to talk with him. As they entered the sacristy, the substitute father wasted no time with small talk and started to relate what had happened to Father Samuel, not forgetting the smallest details—even the desperate screams of Father Samuel as his body was caught in flames.

"Father Samuel has second and first degree burns and his body looks terrible—he nearly died. Imagine that? The irony of fate!"

"How so?" asked Isabel.

"Well, everyone knows that the inquisitor is the person who condemns people who make use of witchcraft by burning them at the stake. The irony is that he himself almost had the same end. God forgive me for thinking this way, after all the father only condemns heretics after receiving superior divine order. Indeed, this is just a careless comment—I'm not here to judge anyone, least of all Father Samuel."

Elizabeth felt horrified by what she had just heard and couldn't stop thinking of Helen. She could hear Helen's painful screams and she felt ill. Her conscious was heavy with remorse and guilt as she recalled that tragic day. These thoughts gave way to fear, a strong fear that she was being punished by God. The father continued:

"So, we called the doctor and he stayed at his side for two days straight putting healing pads on the burns until he felt father was out of danger. One day we left Father Samuel alone for only a few minutes while we were having dinner when we heard him screaming. You can't imagine the terror in his voice! We ran as fast as we could to his room and when we opened the door we nearly fainted at the sight. At this moment, a cat jumped out of father Samuel's bed and ran out the door through our legs. Father Samuel's body was covered with scratches and his eyeballs appeared to be hanging as if the cat had tried to tear them out. It was diabolical, and I will never forget that scene of horror!"

Both mother and daughter covered their eyes immediately, as such was the emotion they felt upon hearing the story about the cat. They would like to have asked more about the animal, but neither had the courage to do so as they recalled the night Damastor died. Isabel then lost control. As he noticed how shaken both women were, the father went to fetch them a glass of water. He returned quickly with the water, and waited a few minutes until both felt better before he continued to talk.

"His screams of pain were maddening. For two nights, and two days he roared nonstop. It seems that the pain has subsided, but he can't see nor talk any longer."

"What?" asked Elizabeth in disbelief.

"Yes, he is blind and deaf. It is very sad to say, but he looks like a monster, no one wants to go near him. His wounds won't heal and they smell terribly. We place his food by him and leave the room as soon as we can. His odor is so strong that we can't bear to stay in the room. It's like his body is decomposing from the inside out. Now you know what happened that day. This tragedy shook us. Until now we still don't know where that cat came from and why he tormented Father Samuel. But God has an explanation for everything—the only thing left is to pray and ask him to feel pity for Father Samuel, because this is too much suffering for a human being to endure."

A silence descended upon the sacristy room as the two women stood there in shock. Elizabeth had stopped talking. A little later, she got up and helped Isabel who nearly fainted. She called Sebastian and asked him to take them out of there at once.

During the way back home, Elizabeth thought over the words of the father about how a person should not have to endure that much pain. How many people had been burned alive because of Father Samuel? How many people were tortured by him until death? Yes, it was punishment, she was sure of that. It was God's punishment. His suffering was a way for him to remember the many acts of cruelty he had practiced through the years against other people, using his authority and power, speaking always in the name of God, using God as a shield for his atrocities. As she pondered all of this, Elizabeth came to the conclusion that she too one day would have to pay for her past acts. *"I think that I have already started to pay. How* can I now judge Father Samuel? At least he acted in the name of God. But me? I acted solely in the name of vanity and prejudice."

She felt sure that everything that had happened to her family was her fault. Elizabeth woke up everyday expecting a new tragedy, and at night had nightmares that always included Helen's dark, hateful eyes.

No one noticed when the carriage pulled up at home. Isabel was still in a state of shock, with empty eyes, lifeless and possessed by fear. Sebastian commented that he had heard about the accident with Father Samuel from a nun, but he couldn't understand the agony that creased his mother and sister's faces. Angrily, Elizabeth asked him to stop talking, and take his sister to her bedroom and call a doctor immediately after settling her. The Werck's family matriarch was crushed. On her way to her bedroom she saw Louiza and Nestor in the stairway.

"Is Leonora better?" she asked.

"Yes, mother," replied Louiza.

"But what happened? Your face..." Louiza continued.

"I'll tell you later, but now please have someone look after Isabel as she is not well. I'm going to rest for a little while and we can talk more over dinner."

Elizabeth then left, leaving the two siblings worried and at a loss.

"Wow Nestor, I didn't like a bit the look of our mother. I fathom that something serious has happened, don't you think?"

"I think so, she looked shaken. Well, I'll go check on Isabel, if you need me, just call me," and Nestor walked away.

At dinner time, Elizabeth told everyone what had happened to Father Samuel. The news brought great sadness to all, including Leonora. True, she didn't like Father Samuel but the tragedy was so great that she felt compassion toward him.

Two days went by, and Leonora couldn't stop thinking about her guardian angel. She hadn't told anyone about him—keeping the secret to herself. She wanted desperately to go to the grotto and was anxiously awaiting the first opportunity. Meanwhile, Isabel was still ill. The events of the past days compromised her already fragile health even more. Several doctors came to try to restore her health, but to no avail. The final diagnosis pointed to her emotional state as the source of her illness, but they complained that without the patient's cooperation little could be done to try to get her out of such a depressive state.

Isabel's heart was infected with a number of bitter life events, starting with being abandoned by her husband in the prime of her youth, then becoming handicapped during the birth of her child, and above all the fact that she didn't accept Leonora as a daughter. All of this dimmed the light of her soul. Leonora instinctively knew that her mother rejected her; she had known this all along. This feeling caused her great sadness, and at times, hate. Despite all of this, Leonora was concerned about her mother's health knowing that unless her mother found the desire to do so, she wouldn't live much longer.

Sometimes, Leonora would go to her mother's room in an attempt to cheer her up, but Isabel would not even look at her daughter, for she was afraid of Leonora's eyes. Unfortunately, even these simple acts of caring by Leonora repulsed Isabel. Leonora even cried a few times due to her mother's cold behavior. Louiza tried to talk to Isabel about this, but no one in the family could change her feelings about her daughter.

Tonight was quite warm and the family was outside drinking refreshments as they hadn't done in a while. The family was all together. Leonora kept them laughing with her jokes and stories, except of course for her mother. A few hours later, Isabel, who hadn't spoken for days, surprised everyone with a whisper that came out with great difficulty.

"I want to request something", she started, "in case I pass away I want you to take Leonora to live with her father in Italy."

Everyone rose to their feet surprised by both her request and the fact that she had started to speak again. Leonora nearly choked on a piece of cake.

"My daughter, what are you saying? This is craziness, besides you are not going to die now."

"Mother, listen to me! Take her far, far away from here!"

Nestor was horrified. He couldn't accept or respect his sister's request and indignantly interjected:

"How can you do that Isabel to your own daughter? You know full well that her father never cared for her, and that I've always been her real father. I'll never permit this nonsense!"

At this point Leonora had tears coming down her face and struggled to get the words out:

"Why mother? Why do you want to take me away from everyone here? You want to separate me from my uncle, place me far away from Uncle Nestor. That's the reason, isn't it? You should know that neither you, nor anybody else will ever separate us. I have already told all of you this but you seem not to believe my words, isn't this so? You can die in peace or in turmoil but I won't leave this house without Uncle Nestor!"

Leonora's voice was filled with hate and Nestor impulsively asked her to shut up.

"Never again do I want to see you speaking in this manner, do you understand me? ... Never!"

Leonora immediately ran to her bedroom with eyes spitting fire. Once more, Isabel had caused the fight between them. She was shaking with hate and her eyes were diabolical. *"I'll take care of this situation,"* she thought.

Not long after, each of the Werck family members went to sleep. There was no more reason for them to stay up to continue the conversation. Isabel was not feeling well and throughout the night she shivered. Leonora was wide awake and from her bedroom she could witness the moaning of her mother's suffering. In the middle of the night, she picked up her cat and walked toward her mother's bedroom. Holding her cat, she slowly opened the door, approached Isabel, and whispered in her ears.

"Mother, wake up, look who I brought to spend the night with you."

Isabel turned over to look at the cat and met Leonora's spiteful stare.

"Look how beautiful he is, mother. You know, this is the cat that made grandpa and Father Samuel die… now he wants to take you. I didn't want this, but you don't like me and that makes him very sad."

Isabel tried to cry out for help but only faint sounds came from her mouth.

"No, Leonora, take him away."

With frail hands and arms, she tried in vain to move the cat away. Next, Leonora threw him at her lap. Isabel became so horrified that her heart gave out and she died with her eyes wide open asking for help.

It was dawn when everyone heard a loud scream coming from Isabel's room. A maid had found her dead and the look on Isabel's face made the maid scream even louder. Another tragedy had beset the family.

A few hours went by… Elizabeth was at her daughter's viewing, utterly destroyed. From dawn until now it appeared she had aged 10 years. Her hair had already lost the beauty it once had but these events had turned it completely gray.

Time kept passing and a week later Leonora still appeared to be devastated with her mother's death or at least that was the impression she wanted to convey to others. This nice morning, she rose from bed early with the desire to visit her guardian angel at the cave and tell him all that had happened, and at the same time assure him that none of it was her fault. In Leonora's dreams Bartholomew talked to her and pleaded with her to ask for God's forgiveness and to pray for her soul and the soul of everyone who had already passed away. These thoughts of Bartholomew were interrupted when she saw Nestor.

"Uncle Nestor, you won't let anyone take me away from here, will you? A letter from my father arrived, but grandma didn't comment on it. Do you think he wants me back?"

"Don't worry, it's nothing like that, he just wrote to show the family his condolences for your mother's death."

"Oh, what a relief!"

"I thought grandma was hiding something from me. I feel better now—I think I'll go for a walk."

Nestor gave a lingering kiss to Leonora's cheek. A passion possessed his body when his lips touched her face. As soon as he became aware of his feelings, he quickly stepped away.

"What happened Uncle Nestor? Your face is red."

"Nothing, it's the heat. I think today will be a very hot one, so be careful and don't go too far."

"Okay," replied Leonora, and she left feeling so elated that she started to sing.

Nestor observed her as she moved away and thought: *"She's becoming a young lady and shortly will turn fifteen. Time really flies, just the other day she was a child. I need to have a conversation with her to try to explain that she's now a young lady."*

Leonora was anxious to arrive at the grotto. Deep down, she felt regret for her thoughts and actions, but she couldn't find it within her to blame herself entirely for the tragedy that had unfolded. In the end, she excused herself because she believed that everyone had deserved to die. By this time, she knew the way to the grotto by heart, so as she got closer she ran to her destination without fear of getting hurt in the rocks. Her excitement was such that she didn't even notice that her arm was lightly bleeding and as she arrived close to the table she promptly called for her angel:

"Angel Bartholomew, I'm here, where are you?"

She turned to the corner where he often stood but it was empty, so she called him for a second time. When she turned back to the table, there he was, sitting still like a decorative piece, a statue.

"I'm very sad for you. With all of your hate, you caused the death of two people. You were in the wrong, Leonora. How can I make you understand that you can't act this way?"

"No, I am not wrong. You think you know it all, but you don't. They were mean. Only I know who they truly were."

"It's not your place to judge, that is God's job, replied Bartholomew. Only he knows what we do and don't deserve, and it's Him who decides when it's time for us to go, not you!"

"But angel, I can't control myself. This is stronger than me. I often have one thought, a good thought but then I do the opposite, it's like a force much greater than I am—a demon that takes over my will."

"This force, my child, is called hate. You will have to dominate it otherwise later on you will have to sit a very difficult judgment."

"What sort of judgment?" asked Leonora.

"The weighing of your soul will be one teetering between the force of love and the force of hate," replied Bartholomew.

"Bartholomew, tell me, which force is the strongest?" asked Leonora curiously.

"You alone will give me this answer, one day" said Bartholomew.

"I don't understand it, so please help me. I don't want to kill anybody else, or rather I don't want to wish anyone dead."

"You have plenty to learn, come on over and sit close to me. We'll start with the first lesson now."

Bartholomew talked for a stretch with Leonora listening attentively and interrupting only a few times with questions. What sparked her curiosity most was his talk about reincarnation. Once again, he tried to explain calmly but Leonora was still too young to fully understand it, so he opted for a simple introduction to the subject.

Leonora had been brought up with the principles of the Catholic Church, so the world of spirits as a new way to understand the events of life was still confusing to her. At this point, she didn't know what to believe.

"Angel, which one should I believe—your words or the words of the Bible?"

"Both, but only later will you choose which one to believe more."

"Do you mean that people who die are born again?"

"Yes, do you understand now what reincarnation is? ... And why we should follow the teachings of God?"

"I think so. If I sin too much in this life, I will pay for my mistakes when I return."

"Yes, more or less like that. But this entire process is much more than just the accounting of mistakes each of us has made."

"The bible says that we all come from dust and to dust we return. Religions differ one from the other, isn't that so angel?"

"More or less, what really matters is that they all speak of God, that's what's most important. Now that you believe in God, think about his son Jesus, and learn to forgive like he forgave those who condemned him to die on the cross."

Leonora got up, pleased with what she had heard. She was impressed by her guardian angel's wisdom and above all the calm and tranquility in which he spoke. This peaceful and loving way to teach her, was well suited to her spirit.

"I'm going to go now, Bartholomew. Everyone at the house is likely worried by my absence."

"That's all right, but remember to fight against hate. Never allow hate to take you over and never forget my words. We will now spend a period of time without talking directly, but when you feel any weakness all you have to do is to think of me because I will be helping you and talking to you through your thoughts and dreams."

"Okay, go with God, Bartholomew."

Her own words surprised her. That was the first time she had mentioned God and it had come from her heart.

Bartholomew smiled and replied, "Go with him, my poor child."

For five years, the Werck family experienced a period of calm where no tragedies befell them. Louiza was still in charge of taking care of Leonora. She was an attentive aunt who always looked over her niece's school work. Leonora had already shown signs of being an intelligent woman. In the meantime, Sebastian got married and moved to Paris where he lived with his wife. Once a year, though, he returned to visit the family and to share with them end of year festivities. He always brought many gifts to Leonora who now was a beautiful woman and very preoccupied with her appearance.

As for Nestor, he was taking good care of the family business that was prospering and growing. At the same time, he kept observing the development of Leonora who surprised him daily by looking more and more like the only woman he had ever loved. Leonora was truly the spitting image of Helen, which troubled Elizabeth who was spending more and more time locked in her bedroom to avoid Leonora's presence. Every time Leonora went to visit her, she pretended to be asleep and this situation was worsening. Nestor and Louiza were running out of excuses to justify

Elizabeth's behavior and Leonora was deeply saddened by her grandmother's rejection.

Nature doesn't skip steps, in the same way, our weaknesses will not disappear overnight. God who loves us unconditionally and in his mercy always interferes in our favor supporting us in our journey. He sends us help through our protective friends, who whisper advice and warning in our hearts, but we have in our hands the power to listen to or ignore them. This is free will.

To change our attitudes is not an easy process because we need to learn about ourselves and the laws of the universe, so that through our own efforts we can control our emotions, which are sometimes beyond our comprehension.

The different situations that occur in our lives are divine blessings to try and test our faith, and over time, through love and pain we become stronger and win over our weaknesses as we follow God's words. At any point in our lives, an honest prayer, the one that comes from deep within our hearts, is a divine sign that was given to us so that we can feel the presence of God and make the best choice in each situation.

Leonora, a child with extreme and antagonistic feelings, can't comprehend the reasons for the hate she feels but she knows that when these negative emotions arise they lead to suffering and the death of people whom she both hates and loves.

God, with all his love, sent her a guardian angel to teach her about the laws of life and forgiveness, and little by little he plants in her heart seeds of goodness. The time required for these seeds to grow and fill Leonora's soul with forgiveness will depend on her effort to conquer hate and allow only love live in her heart.

Chapter 4 – Secrets Revealed

February 19, 1525

It was Leonora's 15th birthday. The whole household was preparing for a grand celebration. Nestor ordered the family to throw the most beautiful party that the neighborhood would ever see. There was no prouder uncle and his niece was so stunning that all the other girls in her age envied her.

Everyone in the family waited for Sebastian's arrival at his niece's party. As it was such a special day, Elizabeth decided to leave her bedroom to help Louiza, who was organizing the festivity. Leonora was pleased to see her grandmother in such good spirits and helping Louiza.

"Grandmother, I'm thrilled to see you here with us! I was afraid you wouldn't join us."

"I am very happy too, my grandchild, after all today is a very special day. I have a gift for you in my bedroom—go fetch it."

Leonora kissed her, and went to get her gift. She returned holding a very beautiful Bible, with a most expensive binding and gold plated cover.

"Thank you grandmother, I love your gift."

"It's for your use. You will find wise words on those pages, and I have no doubt that they will truly guide you for the rest of your life."

"Of course grandmother I will read a passage every night—I promise!"

"Who will celebrate Mass, Louiza? Have you invited the priest?"

"Yes mother, the altar looks amazing—walk out to the garden and give me your opinion."

They were all happy that day—there was peace in the air which left Elizabeth worried and reflective:

"We haven't had peace for a long time. I can feel a hot breeze; it feels like the sign of a bad omen. I am really not happy about this. Lord, have pity on me for I can no longer cope with anymore misfortune. Forgive me, Lord, and keep my family away from harm."

Elizabeth took advantage of this holy place and prayed. She was really uncomfortable with the surrounding serenity. She felt undeserving to have peace in her family.

Everything was ready for the grand celebration with only two hours left before the guests would start to arrive. Sebastian should have already arrived, but was late. Louiza sent Leonora to get changed and the others went to do the same. Everything was in place—they only had to wait for the party.

Leonora was in her room getting ready. Her aunt had ordered her dress from Paris—it was the most beautiful thing Leonora had ever seen. She was delighted with her dress. There were small pearls embroidered around the whole neckline, which was very daring and left the whole neck and part of her beautiful bosom exposed. The dress was made of white tulle and ivory lace, which contrasted with her dark, shiny, bouncy brown hair. Leonora put on a very small tiara, adorned with pearls, so her hair would not come undone. She had just put on her dress when someone knocked on her door.

"Come in" said Leonora.

It was Nestor, who carried something hidden in his hand.

"Uncle Nestor, it is great that you are here! Could you give me a hand with my dress?" She turned around so that he could button it up. There were many small buttons which went from her waist to her shoulders.

"How many buttons!" exclaimed Nestor.

"But you are gorgeous, my niece, and no other woman will compare to your beauty tonight."

Leonora felt very flattered when Nestor praised her beauty. She transformed herself immediately.

"Now I will put on my gift around your neck."

Nestor put her hair up to make it easier, the scent of Eau de Cologne penetrated his nostrils. He was completely inebriated, so he came closer in order to better smell the perfume. Leonora, who could already feel his breath very close to her hair, placed herself closer to his body.

Nestor was putting the necklace, made of diamonds and pearls, over her neck—a heat came over his body. He was not able to resist her body so close to his. So, taking Leonora by her hands, he brought her even closer. Unable to control his emotions, which at that moment were stronger than his will, he started to kiss her back, her neck. He had completely lost control while Leonora was delighted and whispered softly:

"Nestor, I love you… love you very much."

At that moment, Leonora turned slowly so that her lips met his. Nestor could not think. That plump mouth touching his made him go completely crazy. Leonora's dress was still open and Nestor caressed her back.

"My goodness, I love you so much Helen."

Leonora's heart stopped when she heard that name. She tried to say something, but Nestor was kissing her lips so lost in pleasure, that all was left for her to do was to return that kiss, forgetting the name he had mentioned. The two were almost lost when, suddenly, Louiza came in. She was speechless, motionless, her eyes wide open. She couldn't believe what she had just witnessed. Few seconds later, as she recovered herself from shock, she screamed:

"Nestor, stop it right now! Have you gone insane?"

Both of them, unaware of her presence, jumped back, separating their bodies, and still trembling with emotion stood before her.

"How could you, Nestor? I don't understand what is happening here… you are a level-headed man, and Leonora is like your daughter."

Louiza was utterly disappointed with her brother—she never expected such behavior from him. She knew of Leonora's love for Nestor. She could not imagine him acting in that manner; he had always acted responsibly towards her and she was indeed still a child.

"I am not your daughter!" cried Leonora.

Nestor was so confused. He did not understand how he could have behaved in such an uncontrollable manner. His emotions were still so intense that he could barely speak. He sat on a chair, placing his hands over his face, maybe in order not to face his sister, who, totally incensed, wouldn't stop talking.

Leonora started to change. As Louiza spoke about sending her to Paris, that they couldn't be in the same house any longer—Leonora's eyes darkened into evil.

"Shut up!" She said to her aunt.

"I am not going anywhere, neither will Nestor. We love each other, don't we? This is love!"

"No, no!" cried Louiza. "It is not possible. Nestor, say something, please!"

Nestor raised his eyes and gazed at Leonora, and at that moment he was certain that Leonora was Helen.

"I am going crazy, that can't be... Helen died."

He spoke so loudly that Elizabeth could hear his words in her bedroom. Her heart raced for her premonitions were coming true. She ran to Leonora's room. When she was near the door, she heard her son speaking:

"I couldn't resist Louiza. She is Helen—I am sure of it. Look at Leonora and tell me who you see. Now I understand my feelings for Leonora and much more. I fought myself, knowing that I couldn't love her, but my feelings are stronger than reason."

Nestor was suddenly interrupted by Leonora. She was feeling very jealous of this Helen. He spoke of her so lovingly.

"Stop it, Uncle Nestor! Stop calling me that. Who is Helen, who are you talking about?"

Louiza looked at her eyes and was lost for words. Leonora did not look like herself, but like a different person. Louiza did not know Helen very well, neither was she there on the day of her death, otherwise she would have never forgotten the look in her eyes. She stared at her brother not knowing what to say. Elizabeth then decided to enter the room, as if she knew or had heard nothing.

"Leonora, aren't you ready yet? Come on my darling, let's finish getting ready."

Walking towards Leonora, she made sure she turned her grandchild away, so not to look directly into her eyes.

"And the two of you, what are you doing here? Go downstairs, as the guests are already arriving. Your brother has just arrived, go welcome him, as I finish getting Leonora ready."

Nestor couldn't stand up. Louiza approached to help him so that their mother didn't notice anything. He was completely decimated. Leonora looked at Louiza as well, with eyes sparkling with anger, she knew Louiza would do anything to separate them and she wouldn't let that happen.

Sebastian had already made his wife and sister-in-law, who had traveled with him to spend some days in the countryside, comfortable. He started to ask about everyone when Louiza and Nestor entered and welcomed him.

"How are you, Sebastian?"

Louiza embraced him tight, inquiring about his wife and Nestor was next, doing the same.

"She is getting changed for the party—we have just arrived. I brought my sister-in-law alone to spend some days with us. You will meet her soon—she is a charming person, very beautiful, and I am sure you will like her, Nestor."

Louiza glanced at Nestor with a look of complicity, as if saying: this is the solution to your problem.

"How great Sebastian, Nestor really needs to meet a woman who can end his days as a bachelor. Who knows it might be her?"

"Her name is Rose and she is 21, lives in Paris with her parents, and is very accomplished and intelligent. I am sure everybody will like her. But where is the birthday girl? I want to give her my gift and a big hug."

"She is coming. She is finishing getting ready and will be here shortly."

"Well, we have to welcome the guests. Come Nestor, come and help me."

Moving away from Sebastian and walking towards the guests, Louiza whispered in Nestor's ear:

"Please Nestor change your expression, so nobody will notice that something serious is happening."

"I can't Louiza, everything is very confusing in my heart, how could I act like that towards Leonora! She is like a daughter to me—I have always treated her like one. But I love her a lot, desperately. I know that I am mad, on fire, and I cannot control this feeling. Only today did I become aware of this—it, it was a shock."

"Nestor you need to do something to put a stop to this—you know that nothing can happen between the two of you. You need to meet a woman, get married and leave as soon as possible. Do you understand the seriousness of this? Leonora is still a child. If Isabel were alive, she would die from grief knowing of your love for her daughter. As far as your feelings, don't waste your time with nonsense—it's impossible she is Helen. You are delirious, brother. You know it can only be a hallucination. Helen is dead!"

"Stop, Louiza! I don't wish to listen to anything else—leave me alone for a moment. I can't think straight—you don't stop talking. I know I am wrong. I will do something. You can relax, but for now don't say anything else."

Elizabeth was coming down the stairs with Leonora to greet the guests. She was dazzling, resembling a princess with that dress and the necklace that shone upon her neck. When Nestor saw her he was hypnotized once again. Leonora couldn't stop staring at him—she did it with so much love that he blushed. Desperate not to let anybody notice him, he quickly left the house in the direction of the garden, deserting everyone in the ballroom. Leonora was about to chase him when Louiza took her by her arm and said:

"Come Leonora, let's greet your guests who are waiting for you."

Sebastian arrived with his wife and sister-in-law. As he approached them, he kissed Leonora and introduced Rose.

"Sister-in-law, this is Leonora! Leonora, this is Rose, who has journeyed here for a period of rest in our home. She needs a break from the city and I hope that you two become good friends."

Leonora looked at her up and down—she didn't like the idea of having her there at all. She found Rose too beautiful and elegant, a real woman next to her. This made her very jealous. *"I wouldn't want*

Nestor to meet her." That's what Leonora thought, but, very politely, said:

"Nice to meet you, miss. I don't think you will enjoy it here because you are used to city life and in the countryside there is nothing to see and, besides, you will have to be careful when you go out, as we have many snakes around here."

"Don't exaggerate, Leonora!" said Sebastian, "It's not like that, Rose, there aren't as many snakes as in the past, Leonora is joking with you."

"Yes, I am," answered Leonora, a little upset with Sebastian.

Rose noticed that Leonora didn't like her and couldn't understand the reason for her hostility but she was too young for Rose to be concerned about.

Leonora went to meet the other guests. It was almost time for Mass. The priest has just arrived when Elizabeth walked towards him and said:

"Father! How wonderful that you are here! You have no idea how pained I was by the death of the Inquisitor. As you must know, my daughter became seriously ill and died. This is the reason why I couldn't come to either Samuel's burial or Mass. Since Isabel's death I have been very poorly. Too many blows for this old woman, one after another. I hope you forgive my absence."

"It is all right, my child, I was aware of your troubles and I am sorry. Oh, before I forget, I have with me a letter from the Inquisitor, who asked me to hand it to you before he died. So many things have happened. God forgive me, I only remember it now."

"A letter for me? But it has been four years and only now you let me know of the existence of this letter."

"My apologies Lady, but many things happened at the church after Samuel's death. I will bring the letter tomorrow and will tell you the reasons that led me to forget about it."

Elizabeth was very curious about the content of the letter; she could not imagine what the priest wrote to her, but, at the same time, knew it was something serious.

All the guests were in the garden, where the altar had been assembled for the Mass. During the whole ceremony Leonora put her heart into her praying, and she slowly calmed down. Her gaze was mellow, having returned to normal. There were moments in which she thought hard about her angel Bartholomew, whom she hadn't seen for a long time. But every time she kept still, she could see his image and talk to him mentally:

"My friend, I need your help, I don't want to feel anger, but how can I avoid it? Aunt Louiza is going

to try to take Uncle Nestor from me. I won't be able to cope with that! Help me, don't let this happen to me."

Leonora was so lost in her thoughts that she did not notice the priest had already finished and that everyone waited for her to start the ball, that would be opened by her dancing the first waltz with Nestor. The ballroom was very well decorated—lit by candles spread from one end to the other. The lighting made the moment seem like a dream to Leonora. When they embraced, holding each other tightly, both closed their eyes and allowed themselves to be lulled by the sound of the music. Their hearts raced so hard that the sound of their beats mixed up with the waltz. Nestor trembled with emotion while Leonora whispered, with her tender voice into his ear:

"Uncle Nestor, I love you, I won't know how to live without you. I know you love me too—don't run away from me. I want you so much. I am crazy about you."

And Leonora gently touched Nestor's neck with her lips, pressing lightly.

Louiza watched Nestor as he tried to control his emotions. She walked towards Sebastian and said:

"Now is your turn Sebastian, go and dance with Leonora."

Gently, he separated the two of them, taking Leonora into his arms. When Nestor, still inebriated by the magic of the moment that he had lived, walked away from Leonora, Louiza went up to him and said:

"Now brother, ask Rose to dance and for goodness sake, control yourself or everyone will notice."

In order to disguise how he was feeling this is exactly what Nestor did. He approached Rose and asked her to dance. With this gesture the other couples joined them. As soon as Leonora noticed that Nestor was dancing with Rose she started to lose her composure. She could not stand watching him with another woman in his arms. Her eyes were already changing... her expression was transforming... her anger already made the atmosphere heavy so great was the disquiet she projected.

Nestor noticed, or rather felt, there was something wrong with Leonora, and looked for her among the couples. As soon as their eyes met he once more saw only Helen. At that moment he stopped dancing and asked for Sebastian to continue the dance with Rose. He went up to his niece. Gently, he took her away from the young man's arms she was dancing with, excused himself, and guided her to the garden. Louiza, who had not stopped looking after them, followed Leonora and Nestor closely, trying to be discrete so people wouldn't notice what she was doing.

Elizabeth had already taken note of everything and was aware that something very dangerous could happen at any moment with the two of them. She quickly followed Louiza, as it would not be very pleasant if anything happened during the party, as it would be seen by everyone. She called to her, but was not heard—her voice easily overwhelmed by the orchestra and chatter of the guests.

Nestor had taken Leonora to a place far away, the storehouse, as he did not wish for anyone to hear them. He was very shaken—he knew that he had Helen in his grasp and wanted to clear this up once and for all. He would end up going crazy and making a big mistake with his niece. It was what he had in mind when he found himself alone with her. He was going to put an end to these hallucinations.

"Now, listen young lady! Will you tell me what's going on with you?"

Nestor was very distressed. He could barely look into Leonora's eyes—he didn't want to see her change into Helen.

"But Uncle Nestor, what are you talking about? I love you, that's all. I can't control the love I feel. I think I've loved you since I was a baby. I cannot imagine life without you by my side. This feeling is stronger than me."

Leonora was in tears; she was also very agitated. She wanted to be calm; to tell him everything that she felt; but just the fact of seeing him dancing with another woman left her deeply jealous.

"You are mine, do you understand, Nestor? No one will take you away from me... I'd rather die than see that happen—so in that case I'll take you away with me!"

Nestor stood still listening to that child talking in such a manner. The woman he knew as a child could never say these things. This could not be Leonora—something was happening beyond his reach and knowledge. He could not comprehend what was happening. When he looked into her eyes, eyes moist with tears, he felt a tingling that came from inside his soul. He was certain at that moment that he was not crazy. The woman in front of him was Helen. He quickly turned away and said:

"Stop that Leonora—this is not you! I don't understand what causes you to say these things, but I know that something supernatural is happening to you—we need to look for help."

"No! I don't need any help, I just need you, don't you see? It is stronger than us. Stop fighting it Nestor. Tell me why we can't be happy? Nothing is preventing us... think carefully."

Louiza had just entered the storehouse and on hearing Leonora said:

"This is your uncle. He has your mother's blood. This would be a sin."

Leonora turned her face toward Louiza with eyes filled with so much anger there was no need for words.

"Liar!" Leonora said.

"You're just like everyone else in this family, as bad as your father, he was a bastard. You know very well I am not Isabel's real daughter. It was you who came up with this pretense—I am the maid's daughter who died that night. Your blood doesn't run through my veins... nothing prevents our love and you know that very well."

Nestor looked at his sister, he could not understand what Leonora was saying, and Louiza did not know how she had found out the family's great secret. Louiza was completely pale with Leonora's revelation and at the same time intrigued to know how she had found out about her birth. She made an epic effort not to faint.

"Talk to me, say something! Is it true what Leonora is saying?"

Elizabeth, who came crying into the storehouse, answered for Louiza:

"Yes, it is, my son, but Louiza is not to blame, she just wanted to help that child who had become an orphan as soon as she was born. Isabel's son died the moment he was born. Our only sin was to switch the babies so that nobody suffered even more. You were not at home that night, so we decided not to tell you anything. We thought that would be for the best. The fewer people knew about it the better our chances to keep it a secret."

Elizabeth then asked Leonora:

"What about you my grandchild, how did you find out?"

"I've always known—I don't know how—I don't have a recollection of my birth, but I knew my blood was not the same that runs through your veins."

Louiza could hardly stand up so her mother supported her on her shoulder.

"Don't be like that Louiza. It is over. We can be at peace now—our secret has been revealed. Our biggest worry was for you Leonora, but, look at the irony of fate, you were the one to out our secret."

Louiza looked into those eyes that wouldn't stop staring at her and said:

"I have always loved you as if you were my own child—I never let you feel as if you were not loved by us—I spent many nights awake keeping watch over you, as your health was very fragile. You cannot tell me now that none of this is important. You are not that hard."

As Louiza spoke, it was clear that her love for Leonora was that of a mother's, and her niece was sure of this and so moved, said:

"I love you too, auntie. I do remember you taking me into your arms as soon as my real mother passed away. I even remember your words and I am very thankful for that. But, if you love me the way you say you do, don't take Nestor away from me. I wouldn't be able to forgive you for that."

Nestor was much shaken, and even more confused with everything that Leonora had just revealed: her memories from when she was a baby; her feeling of ownership towards him; her change when she lost control of her emotions; all the love she had for him; and the anger she showed towards his family. Without a word he left the storehouse, head down, wishing to be left alone. The three women, still exchanging glances, were lost for words. Leonora said that for her the party was over. She would retire to her bedroom. Upon leaving she asked that they provide an excuse to the guests to justify her leaving the party so early.

Only mother and daughter were left, completely helpless, suffering from all the past memories. Elizabeth, could not cope with so much sadness in her heart, and so much anger in her granddaughter's face. She could not forget the great mistake she had made in the past, and Leonora was a living memory who tormented her day and night. To look at her was to look at Helen—she no longer had any doubt about that.

Sebastian played host till the last guest left. He did not know what had happened, but at his mother's request he stayed until the end of the party playing host. Nestor had disappeared, not returning to the house. The day was dawning when Louiza asked the servants about Nestor and nobody knew of his whereabouts. She was very anxious to talk to him, and at this moment, her mother, who also could not sleep, came downstairs looking for him too.

"Good morning daughter, have you found Nestor?"

"No mother, nobody knows where he is. He has probably gone on one of his long walks to we never know where."

Leonora, who was already awake, hid and listened to their conversation. She had a good idea where Nestor might have gone. She was retiring to her bedroom when she overheard Louiza talking to Elizabeth:

"Mother, we need to convince Nestor to get married, he has to leave this house. I can feel something very bad is about to happen. This woman,

Sebastian's sister-in-law, could be our candidate, what do you think?"

Elizabeth was going to reply when she was abruptly interrupted by Leonora, who was going berserk.

"I don't think you understood me, auntie."

Her tone of voice was low and threatening.

"I was not kidding when I said nobody is going to keep me away from Nestor."

Her eyes were as red as blood. Her expression was really supernatural, as if she was possessed by the devil. Elizabeth spoke:

"Calm down, Leonora, you misunderstood what your aunt meant to say".

"No I didn't. And you, shut up! Have you forgotten you are responsible for all this? Thanks to your wickedness, your social prejudice caused the death of my whole family and made me into a witch! Do you remember, old woman, that because of you I was burnt alive?"

Louiza could not believe her ears, she looked at her mother, not knowing what to think.

"Who is this woman who is in Leonora's body? Who is using her voice to say such evil?" thought Louiza.

"Who are you?" she screamed.

And then she started to shake Leonora, with all her strength, invoking God's name so that this devil would leave her body. Elizabeth was quiet, everything she had said was the pure and honest truth.

"Forgive me!!!" said Elizabeth. "Punish me, if you so wish, but leave my children alone!"

Leonora had returned to being the sweet girl and, as if coming out of a trance, gently said, while crying:

"Stop auntie, you are hurting me."

Leonora run out to the garden and Louiza ran after her, screaming:

"Stop, Leonora, where are you going, stop!"

Leonora, who was faster than Louiza, passed by her on horseback, almost knocking her over on the way. Louiza ran to the stables and ordered her horse to be saddled as soon as possible. The servant was surprised by her request, because they all knew Louiza was afraid of horses. She had not mounted a horse since suffering a bad fall as a child.

"Quick, bring me a horse!"

She left in a rush, trying to catch up with Leonora. She wanted to prevent Leonora from doing something stupid—she was not to blame for what was happening, thought Louiza. And as she galloped off, she screamed her name:

"Leonora! Leonora!"

She was afraid something might happen to Leonora. If something happened to her, she would never forgive herself. Suddenly, a cat crossed in front of the horse, causing the horse to balk, throwing her off. Her vision started to fade, her breathing weakened, until she was gone. Leonora, who had galloped fast after Nestor, was completely in turmoil when her horse reared up and nearly threw her off, and she saw before her the angel Bartholomew.

"Go back Leonora, you need to go back. Your aunt fell off her horse and she needs you."

For a few seconds she doubted whether to go back, but love spoke louder at that moment, and she decided to return. A short while later she found Louiza's body lying on the road. It appeared that she might be dead. Leonora dismounted quickly, and ran towards her and as she approached she could see it really was Louiza on the road. She became very emotional, not able to control herself she threw herself on top of her aunt, and burst into tears crying:

"I love you aunt Louiza! Please don't die… You cannot leave me!"

Elizabeth hearing her daughter had gone out on a horse, woke Sebastian and told him to go after them both. When he arrived he saw the most touching scene of his life. Leonora, calling Louiza as mother, asked her to wake up, not to die, because she really loved her.

"Please, mother, forgive me! I did not mean what I said, I love you, it's true. Wake up, please!"

Sebastian, moved by her pain gently tried to remove her from the top of Louiza's body, saying:

"Come on, Leonora, it's over…"

Sebastian then started to cry. He took his sister in his arms and took her body home. Elizabeth kept checking the entrance gate, waiting, with an aching heart. She sensed a new tragedy was about to happen, but not the death of her daughter. When she caught sight of Sebastian, still very far off, carrying Louiza's body, she let out a cry of pain. It was so deep that those around her felt sorry to see her this way. Her state of anguish and pain was pitiful.

"Oh, God, no! Not my daughter!"

Of all the funerals that had already taken place in that house, this was the saddest one. They all found it hard to accept Louiza's death—she had always been so good. The servants were inconsolable, they truly liked their mistress. Nestor felt responsible and remorse for causing his sister so much heartbreak. He blamed himself and felt that he caused her death. Leonora blamed herself for not having stopped and listened to her urging, when Louiza called to her. She genuinely loved her aunt. There were only two people in that family who were in any position of making Leonora feel affection and true love—Louiza and Nestor.

After this new tragedy, Elizabeth resembled a zombie—her appearance was of pure paralytic suffering. She carried her guilt in silence knowing that if Nestor came to find out she was responsible for Helen's death, he would never forgive her. She could not lose another child at this stage in her life. She would not be able to withstand the anger in his eyes arising from his knowledge of her cowardly actions towards that girl and her family.

Two weeks had passed since that tragic day. There was only sadness in the house. They were all still shaken by Louiza's death. Nestor, who was riddled with guilt, decided to go away for some time. He wanted to be away from Leonora. He would leave with his brother Sebastian to Paris. There was so much sadness in the air that they could hardly breathe—nobody could stand to be in the house any longer. They felt that there was a curse. They only didn't know the reason why.

Leonora remained locked in her room—she didn't wish to talk to anyone, and refused to see even Nestor. That morning Nestor told Elizabeth about his decision, saying he would be back when everything was resolved inside his heart. He could no longer stay there while he felt this love for Leonora, confused with the memories of his two sisters, Louiza and Isabel. Elizabeth understood what he meant and said no more. She kissed her son and thanked him for leaving. She could hardly speak, but very frailly, she mumbled:

"God be with you, my son, don't you worry about me. I will be fine—this was your sister's wish. Write whenever you can—send us news."

Leonora had not noticed the different buzz in the house. She did not know Nestor was about to leave. She couldn't even imagine it. Without her knowledge and with a broken heart, Nestor left. As he went away, he looked at Leonora's closed window and whispered to himself goodbye, thinking:

"I would love to look at your face one more time, but I do this for your own good."

Nestor was certain he was doing the right thing, but he still found it hard to leave. He knew that when Leonora found out he had left, she would not accept him leaving and this worried him, but it was not possible to stay there another minute.

Leonora was a woman now. Even apart the feelings of love flourished deeper between her and Nestor. Neither could clearly understand what was happening—they only felt that it was a love impossible to control.

They did not know it was a re-encounter of two old souls who loved each other deeply and who should have been happy and together in this lifetime—fulfilling what had been planned before they were born.

However, due to Elizabeth's selfishness and bad choices, this union could not be realized. This was the original cause of this family's pain and suffering that led to Helen's extreme and uncontrollable anger. Elizabeth through injustice to Helen had unleashed forces opposed to good—energy to cause sadness and death.

The family went through a difficult and very painful experience, but going through this pain gave them the opportunity for deep reflection which will mark the soul of each of those involved. The past suffering prepared the fields of the future, to sow good and strong seeds for the awakening of love and forgiveness.

Leonora was profoundly shaken as she loved her aunt dearly and found it hard to accept her death for which she felt responsible. For the first time, after so many tragedies, Leonora started a conscious battle between two intense feelings, love and hate.

Chapter 5 - The Separation

Three years had passed—Leonora was eighteen now. She ran the household for her grandmother, who could hardly speak or walk. Nestor hadn't come back. He frequently wrote asking for news and told them what he had been doing in Paris; he ran the family business from there and took the opportunity to study. Leonora read his letters and answered them, always imploring him to return home.

When Leonora learned about Nestor departure to Paris she had become enraged like a caged beast. She blamed everybody, mainly her grandmother, for having influenced his departure. She carried a lot of bitterness and hate in her heart and thus suffered greatly. She missed him so much she could hardly sleep.

During all these years, Leonora tossed and turned during the night, dreaming about Nestor. She called out to him and sometimes screamed his name so loud while sleeping that Elizabeth, in her bedroom, could hear her. When this happened Elizabeth prayed, asking for God to have mercy on that soul who suffered so much for love. She asked to be forgiven for being responsible for creating so much agony and pain. She asked God to take her, and in return bring Leonora and

Nestor some peace—to free them from so much suffering.

Leonora never managed to return to her old self—her eyes never shone gentle and tender again. She screamed at everybody and treated Elizabeth with coldness. The servants were scared of her and felt sorry for the grandmother, being so mistreated—not that Elizabeth had been a good mistress; she had always treated the help with indifference and ignored them when they needed help. She was a cold person who was not moved by the suffering of her servants and the needy, but in spite of such unpleasant remembrances they couldn't help but feel sorry for an old lady who was in so much pain, and who had to pay for her sins.

Leonora tortured Elizabeth day and night with her catty and biting words. She wouldn't leave her alone for a single day, and said she would only give her peace on the day that she brought Nestor home. Leonora always reminded her that she was the one to blame for everything.

The priest sometimes came to see Elizabeth and calm her—but usually only when Leonora wasn't around, having found out through the servants when she was away.

Sometimes Leonora tried to talk to her angel Bartholomew, but it was in vain. She carried so much hate in her heart that she could not get through to him. It made her believe she had been abandoned by all. For this reason, she had not gone to the cave again to look for him, and did not wish to believe in his words any longer.

On the other hand, Bartholomew, no matter how much he tried could not contact Leonora—it was impossible as her mind blocked the communication, thus not allowing him to help her. She tried to convince herself the whole time that the angel and everything else were nothing more than her imagination, that it was simply a child's hallucination. She wanted to believe her convictions were real, she did not want to waiver—the only thing that mattered was to have Nestor back at any price, and not even an imaginary angel would make her change her mind.

Before retiring to her room nightly she would always see Elizabeth, not to check on her but to torment her. Elizabeth suffered in silence—any hate or rancor was shunted aside by the overwhelming guilt she felt. She always looked at Leonora tenderly, in a way that made Leonora regret, at least slightly, the way she treated her grandmother. There were some moments Leonora even managed to be sweet for a few seconds, but something would happen within a few breaths to return all to darkness. It was a feeling beyond Leonora's control. She could feel the sudden change in her spirit and this bothered her a lot because deep down she did not want to behave that way, but she did not know how to control herself and thus remained in conflict, fighting against her conscience.

One morning, Leonora received a letter from Nestor. On opening it she was astounded; she could not believe her eyes; her face started to change—her appearance was of pure joy. She could not contain her happiness. Remarkably, she drifted back to acting as a child—she read and re-read the letter many times. Even the servants were surprised to see how happy she was and were most curious about what Nestor had said in the letter to give her so much pleasure. After some time, convinced it was real, she called everyone to tell them the great news:

"Nestor is coming back and he is probably arriving tomorrow. I want everyone to be ready for his arrival. Get his room ready—open all the windows to air the rooms, well, don't forget anything... don't spare any detail. We are preparing for a party!"

Such was her happiness that, unconsciously she had returned to being Leonora. She went to her grandmother's bedroom to see if Elizabeth were awake, and came in saying:

"Granny, Nestor is coming back! Have you heard what I said? Wake up. Nestor is back!"

Leonora's tears rolled down her cheeks.

Elizabeth shook her head acknowledging it. She was thrilled to see her Leonora back, for since

Nestor had left she could only see Helen—only a very few times was she able to see the face of her granddaughter.

Leonora noticed a smidgen of worry in her look and said:

"Don't be like that; everything will be all right, you'll see. In the letter he states that he should arrive tomorrow, therefore dear granny, let's leave the bed so that the servants can tidy up your room."

Elizabeth, listening to Leonora, thought:

"The tenderness in Leonora's voice is impressive. What malign force is that which manages to make a person change so much. It cannot be Helen, for I've always known her to be gentle and kind, a very religious Catholic. She could not be such a bad and rancorous soul."

While they tidied up her room, observing Leonora, Elizabeth carried on thinking:

"This girl cannot really live without Nestor; I have to admit that her feelings for him are almost to the point of being unhealthy. I think she would go insane if Nestor married."

Leonora was so anxious that night that she could hardly sleep—in vain she tried counting the stars outside her window. She wasn't even hungry—what she most wanted was for the night to be short and to pass quickly. Not noticing that fatigue had taken over she fell asleep for some time during which she had a dream with her angel Bartholomew:

"Leonora!" He called.

"Listen to what I am going to say: I've always been by your side—believe it or not. How can I get through to you if you only have hate in your heart? Listen, whatever happens, my daughter, remember what I told you one day: hate is not you, you are only love. Don't forget this… don't let hate win."

Leonora jumped off her bed with her heart racing. The dream made her ache deep down in her soul—a premonition, maybe something about Nestor.

"I fear Bartholomew is trying to warn me that something is going to happen! He is trying to prevent something bad from happening, but what is it?"

She got up, walked to the window to look at the sky. It was almost daybreak, and the stars indicated that it was going to be a beautiful day. She stood motionless at the window for some time and thought:

"Nestor must be near and soon he will be by my side. Oh Lord, it has been three years since we last saw each other, since aunt Louiza's death. Does he still think of me? Does he still love me? I'm sorry for everything that happened, I didn't want it, I swear I didn't! But please, Lord, don't take him away from me! I won't be able to cope. I know I won't. If I have

*survived to this date, it's because I haven't lost hope—
I knew one day he would come back to me. I don't want
hate in my heart—I just want love, but without Nestor
this is practically impossible!"*

She spent some time looking at the road,
imagining his arrival, when she suddenly had a vision.
It was Louiza, bringing her sister, Leonora's adoptive
mother Isabel. Leonora couldn't believe her eyes. She
waived as if she was calling her. She wanted to run
away from the window but her legs wouldn't obey. She
heard as if a voice inside her spoke:

"We're arriving with Nestor."

She recognized Louiza's voice, it was smooth.
She spoke with a lot of tenderness.

*"Daughter listen to me, learn how to forgive. If
you manage, all of this will be finished. We love you
very much and that's why we're here—try to
remember, make an effort, you need to repent…"*

Leonora couldn't control herself—she started
to cry, calling for Louiza who slowly faded away…

"Aunt Louiza, I love you too, I've always loved
you, I did not want anything to happen… I know you
know I am telling the truth. Sometimes I even confuse
myself. I cannot understand the change in my behavior,
but I tell you, from the bottom of my heart, I love you,
I love my mother Isabel and I love my grandmother."

"This is all very confusing", thought Leonora, *"How can I hate and love at the same time?"*

She became very emotional following the vision of Louiza and Isabel and very sensitive—deeply touched by everything that had happened during that night. The dream with her angel, the vision, the wait for Nestor, everything made Leonora very needy and fragile. All the events made her feel like a lost child—she had a pleading look in her eyes.

Her grandmother noticed Leonora's fragility that morning. Elizabeth looked at her with tenderness and wanted to tell her how beautiful she looked and that she should always be so affectionate because everything would be easier that way. She struggled to say some words of comfort and affection and waived for Leonora to approach her and mumbled:

"Granddaughter, forgive your grandmother, I didn't know what I was doing. I love you very much, as much as I love Nestor, and I long from the bottom of my heart that you are both happy."

It was hard for Elizabeth to speak, but Leonora understood everything she said. With a lot of love, she embraced her grandmother and started to cry.

"I'd like to know what you did to me. I can only remember that you were good to me and I only treated you badly. I'm aware that I need to recall something very serious, but what?"

Elizabeth wanted to speak, but she couldn't, she was very emotional, and started to feel unwell from all the effort.

"Stop grandmother, please don't say anything else, keep calm, I don't want to see you like that."

For the first time Elizabeth felt her real granddaughter, whole, free from any curse in her spirit. Then, she elevated her thought to God, thanking him for a moment of peace in her soul. While she was praying, she said a prayer for Helen's soul to forgive her, to find peace, and to let Leonora's spirit find her way. She prayed for her granddaughter, but she did not know the mysteries of death, she had no knowledge of what reincarnation was, she just thought Leonora's spirit was being tormented by Helen's soul.

At this moment, Elizabeth's greatest concern was Nestor's return—she knew something bad could happen. She put it in God's hands and asked that His will be done, that He show pity on her and Helen. Elizabeth asked that He concede her one grace before she died: that she could confess her crime to Nestor, so she could die in peace. She got lost in her prayers, but would not stop looking at her granddaughter who had stayed by her side. Few minutes later, Leonora asked:

"Why do you look so much at me, grandmother?"

Elizabeth answered with a weak smile, caressing her face. After that, Leonora came very close to Elizabeth and gently started to comb her hair.

"Come on, I want to see you very beautiful. Nestor wouldn't want to see you disheveled, let's put on a nice nightgown and some scented water."

After brushing Elizabeth's hair and applying fragrance to her so she would be ready to greet Nestor, Leonora said:

"I'm going to get changed, so I can look as beautiful as you."

Then, she kissed her grandmother tenderly on her forehead and left. She was very nervous, and could hardly help herself prepare for Nestor. She chose a gorgeous white dress, to go with the state of her soul, white, soft and calm. She let her hair down, which was waist long, and put on a tiara so her hair wouldn't be in her eyes. Lastly she sprinkled on a mild eau de cologne. She was looking at herself on the mirror when the noise of a carriage jarred her from her thoughts.

"That's him!"

She ran to the window to see if she was right. She knew she was, her heart would never deceive her.

Nestor was very nervous, all those years did not make him forget Leonora. He dreamt about her every night, heard her begging in his dreams and read all her letters. He fought hard to resist her calls. Now that he was close to see her again, he shook all over at the thought of going weak—he could not forget the promise he made to himself. He wanted Louiza's soul to rest in peace and he was not going to forget it.

He greeted the servants on entering the house, gave them his coat and baggage, and asked if everything was in order and where his mother and Leonora were. As he entered the small room he looked to the top of the stairs which lead to the bedrooms, and saw Leonora standing there holding on to the banister, in order not to fall, such was her emotion.

They spent a few seconds staring at each other unable to say anything, their emotions etched into their faces, which blushed as the heat moved up their bodies. Nestor had to make a huge effort not to throw himself into Leonora's arms. His desire was to embrace her, kiss her till he couldn't anymore, to finally quench the thirst, kill the overwhelming ache for her that had haunted him during those three years of absence.

Leonora came down very slowly, step by step, without saying a word, she only stared at him. Her eyes spoke for themselves. They said how much she loved him, how much she had suffered with his absence. She was very close to Nestor, who hypnotized by her appearance, couldn't move. With a tender and soft voice Leonora finally said:

"Uncle Nestor, I missed you!"

"I missed you too, Leonora—I couldn't stand being away from the two of you."

He was struggling inside but he couldn't falter.

"You look very beautiful! You haven't lost your childlike charm."

Leonora did not reply. She approached him, touching him with her lips, but Nestor quickly distanced himself, and changing subject, he asked:

"Mother, where is she?"

Nestor didn't look at Leonora anymore, he couldn't...

"She's in her bedroom waiting for you."

Leonora walked away happily, followed by her uncle, toward the bedroom of her grandmother and soon realized that Nestor looked at her full of tenderness and love—enjoying the moment she charmingly turned and called:

"Uncle Nestor!"

Her voice jarred Nestor from the momentary trance he was in, and trying to hide his emotions he replied:

"Yes, niece."

He tried to be cold and formal, but it was really hard to control himself. Leonora understood what he was trying to do. Being a smart girl, she didn't want to frighten him, so she let him treat her that way, without teasing him.

"Don't you think it's best to get changed? Then go see grandma—she's dying to see you. Your belongings are handy and your bath is ready. All you need to do is wash and get changed. I'll order you a light snack while you wait for lunch. Would that be ok?"

"Everything's perfect, my niece, I'll follow your suggestion and then go and see mother."

Leonora followed him with her eyes as he climbed the stairs and noticed how strong he was—his hair was already turning grey, but she found him even more handsome. A few hours later Nestor knocked on the door of his mother's bedroom, saying:

"May I come in?"

"Come in Uncle Nestor! Grandmother is anxious to see you."

Nestor entered the room and went straight to hug his mother. Elizabeth had tears in her eyes and couldn't speak, but she didn't need to—it was clear to see how emotional she was to see her son.

"Don't cry mother, I'm here now. I missed you so much!"

Nestor spent a long time with Elizabeth. He waited for her lunch to be served and told her all the latest news from Paris. He told her about Sebastian and his wife, and mentioned that he would take her there very soon. Elizabeth opened her eyes wide, demonstrating she could not understand how she would be able to go, as she was so ill.

"I'll tell you later what really brought me here and why! You need to rest now. Leonora told me you overdid it and this has made you exhausted. The doctor said that your heart's very weak and that you shouldn't strain yourself. I'm going downstairs for lunch and then I'm going to have a rest, but before dinner I'll return so we can talk some more."

He kissed her on the face, made her comfortable, rearranged her pillow and told her to rest. Leonora watched everything and waited for her uncle to finish so she could order lunch.

"You see it now, right? Grandmother's very frail and we can no longer cope on our own here—her state of health requires special care."

"I know my angel, and that's exactly what I want to talk to you about. We'll talk later."

Lunch was fine and Leonora told him everything that had been happening in town and the state of business. There were moments when Nestor did not even hear what she was saying—he just watched her move as if he were bewitched. His thoughts wandered off, so many recollections. He looked at her hands which gesticulated gently. She looked like a child talking—her tender eyes seemed to shine brighter each time she looked at him. They finished having lunch and went out for a walk in the garden.

"Now, I'm going to rest; I still haven't recovered from the trip. You won't be angry with me if I leave you here alone, will you?"

"Of course not, Uncle Nestor, you do look a little tired, we'll continue our conversation during dinner."

Nestor kissed her gently on the forehead, and at this moment Leonora held his arm and said:

"Aren't I your darling niece anymore?"

"Yes you are, and you know very well that I adore you."

"Why don't you kiss and hug me properly? After such a long time, I thought that you missed me."

"I missed you a lot, Leonora, but I'm tired."

Leonora went up to him, put his arms around her neck, came very close and gently touched his hair and face with her lips, and whispered:

"I nearly died I missed you so much; please don't leave again—I don't think I could cope. Say that you won't leave me. Say something, I beg you!"

"Leonora my angel, things have changed some and you need to understand that you are not a small child anymore. You are a young woman and can no longer act that way towards your uncle."

"But why not? Everybody knows how much I love you. I've never hidden that from anyone. I don't see any problem in hugging you."

Nestor tried to remove his arms from around her neck, he was worn down from having to control himself and about to kiss her. His lips were so close to hers that his legs trembled with desire.

"Please Leonora, stop it!"

Nestor left, he almost ran, leaving Leonora lost in her thoughts and saddened by his reaction. She tried to control herself—she wanted to take it slowly. She would have to be patient—she knew that after Louiza's death Nestor was going to do everything in his power to keep his distance from her, because he still blamed himself for the death of Louiza. When he arrived at his bedroom, Nestor tried to calm down, he could not be so close to Leonora without feeling this strong desire to embrace and kiss her.

"My Lord, I don't know what to do! When we are together what takes place is stronger than any feelings I've ever known. You know I've done everything to remove her from my heart, maybe who knows I've even taken the wrong route, but it was the only one I found at that moment. Please Lord, give me strength! I need to tell the truth to her and my mother. How, how can I tell Leonora that I got married?... Sister, if you can, help me, come to my aid, make Leonora understand it was necessary."

Nestor did not want to see Leonora's look of disappointment; he was afraid of how she would react when she discovered that he had married Rose. In that moment, the marriage to Rose was the only way he found to escape the passion that he felt for his niece. She should see him as an uncle, as before. He could not fall into the temptation of loving her; something that he had promised not to do on his sister's grave. But now that he saw her again, his heart betrayed him. He found himself completely helpless in the face of the revelation he had to make sooner or later, it was just a matter of time.

During those three years while he was away Nestor fooled himself, thinking that he would get over his passion for Leonora, that he would see her with the love of a father, as before. Everything would be seen as nothing more than a misunderstanding on his part and that he would feel nothing but a fraternal love for her. So, he decided to marry Rose, she was a beautiful woman, a good friend, who helped him to forget his remorse from so tragically losing his sister, Louiza. She gave him strength to overcome his pain. Rose was sweet, gentle and she really loved Nestor, she did everything to help him. Although she knew of his love for Leonora, she agreed to marry him.

When Rose learned of his departure, she became very worried; she felt in her heart that it still wasn't the right moment for him to go back. She knew her husband still loved Leonora, but Nestor used the letter he received telling him about his mother's delicate state of health as an argument, a reason to return to his mother's home. He said it made him fear her death. Besides that, he couldn't write about his marriage, he would have to tell everyone personally.

Now Nestor realized Rose was right, he was not ready to see Leonora. He had deluded himself into thinking that he had forgotten her—it simply wasn't true. No sooner had he seen her then the memories came flooding back, and he felt all the love intensely throbbing in his heart. Since then, Nestor called his sisters in his prayers asking for help, because he felt his resolve beginning to waver.

"Oh my God! How am I going to reveal the truth to Leonora without causing her pain?"

Meanwhile Leonora, who had stayed behind in the garden, felt frustrated with her unsuccessful foray. She caressed her cat, which turned up every so often, especially when his owner was sad. As if it understood, its appearance was always at the most appropriate time—when Leonora couldn't get hold of her emotions. At this moment, she fought her inner self, thinking about Bartholomew's words. She tried to control herself in order not to lose her temper.

Leonora told them to saddle her horse——she had decided to go horseback riding in order to make the time pass. She rode for a while, lost in her thoughts, without realizing she was a long distance from the house. She was not paying any attention to which direction she was heading. She only noticed where she was when she saw the rocks from the grotto's entrance——so she followed in its direction.

"Goodness, I hadn't noticed where I was heading!"

"I might as well go in—it has been a long time since I last came here. Am I going to see Bartholomew? I would very much like to see him again."

Leonora was not a child anymore and found it challenging to go through the narrow space between the rocks. She tried to squeeze through the small space that led to the interior of the grotto. With great effort she managed, and found herself inside her childhood hide-out. She tried to remember the moments of the past when she used to talk to her angel.

She had learned a lot from her angel about spiritual truths. With this spiritual grounding she found it easy to see spirits and talk with them, as when she had seen Louiza and Isabel. At first, she felt fear but then remembered her conversations with her angel and calmed herself. It became easier each time to accept spiritual manifestations, like spirits' appearances.

She walked towards the altar of stone, which she had called a table when she was a child. Now she could see clearly that it was an altar, man-made, probably by Nestor; but she still could not understand its purpose. She smoothed the surface, hoping for something to happen. She was in doubt if she would really see Bartholomew—perhaps he was only a vision from her childhood. She was almost giving up, when she saw directly in front of her the old Bartholomew, as always, sitting and looking at the floor.

"It's true, then! You are not the fruit of a child's fertile imagination."

"You wished it, Leonora, you did everything to believe so, but you know very well I am real for you. I never stopped being by your side, even when you did not want to believe. The only way I found to reach your thoughts was through your dreams."

"And the vision I had of my mother and aunt Louiza, was it real as well?"

"You know it was, don't fool yourself, Leonora. You are aware of your power, you just don't want to remember. This internal struggle of yours is only undermining your development and the enlightenment needed for you to regret your actions."

"Please Bartholomew, help me. I do not wish to feel this hate. I want to try to exert control over my will; I do not wish for any more tragedy to take place—please help me remember what I need to know..."

"Thank goodness my child that you are now thinking more positively—this is a good sign. Pray my darling and read a lot; I'll recommend books that talk about the spiritual world, which can help you better understand your karma. For only through reading will you'll remember and recognize your mistakes. I'll always be here, ready to help you."

On saying that, Bartholomew informed her of the names of the books she should read and where to find them. They talked a little more. When Leonora said goodbye, it was getting late and would soon be dark.

"May God be with you, my child, have faith and don't forget, let love be your guide."

"Goodbye angel, thank you very much. I'll be back as soon as possible."

Leonora rode fast, the afternoon was gone, and the night was drawing in. It was dangerous to be in such a remote area alone at night and there were some kilometers to cover in order to reach home. She was very apprehensive; she had never been alone at night on a country road and started to hear some strange noises.

She couldn't gallop any longer, as it was almost impossible to see anything ahead. She was breaking out in a cold sweat—there was something bothering her as if something or someone was following her. Her sixth sense alerted her about the danger.

Nestor, worried about Leonora's delay, had asked the servants where she might be, but they did not know. He went to his mother's room to see if he could find anything out, but when he opened the door, and saw that she was deeply asleep he decided not to wake her.

He went to the garden and stood a few minutes looking at the gate. He was very impatient; he couldn't stay still and not do anything so he ordered the servants to prepare his horse. He would look for her. As if by instinct, or love, his heart told him the direction to take and without hesitation he went straight to the grotto.

Something guided him there. The night was really dark and along the country road he called out her name—Leonora. Every so often he stayed still, trying to see something in the darkness. The more time passed without finding her, the more his worries grew—causing him to become more nervous.

"Oh Lord, please don't let anything bad happen to her. I will not forgive myself. I know she was unhappy with me—I cannot lose her... Leonora! Leonora! Where are you?"

He persisted on screaming, he sounded like an insane person, when in the silence of the night he heard a light moan. The noise wasn't too far away, therefore he started to shout:

"Leonora, is that you? My love, answer for the love of God!"

He continued to hear the moaning and drawing very close to some rocks he spotted her lying on the road. She looked very hurt. Nestor let out a cry of happiness when he saw it was her.

"Leonora! Thank God I've found you, my love."

He ran to pick her up in his arms and could see she was very hurt, with cuts and bruises all over her body.

"Be still, my love, let's go home and I'll take care of your wounds."

He picked her up very gently, as he was afraid of hurting her even more. Leonora, seeing an opportunity, even though somewhat dizzy, took advantage of the situation and started to over dramatize her condition. She moaned in pain and cried on his shoulders which left Nestor even more worried about her physical state.

"Maybe you broke a leg or an arm? Leonora, where does it hurt, tell me, show me."

"Uncle Nestor, the pain is all over my body, especially in my leg. I can't walk."

"You must have broken something. I will carry you very carefully and will not let you hurt yourself again. Trust me."

He made her comfortable on his horse and took the animal by the reins with plenty of care walking slowly alongside the horse trying not to jar Leonora too much along the way. He constantly asked if everything was okay—if she could cope a little longer. He reassured her that they would soon be home. When he saw the castle, he started to shout for the servants to come and help him.

"What is it, sir? What happened?"

"The miss is very hurt. Run, go fetch the doctor. Take the horse. I'll carry her inside. Don't make any noise—I don't want my mother to become agitated. Don't tell her anything."

Nestor took Leonora straight to a room, far from Elizabeth's room—as he didn't want his mother to hear Leonora moaning. His mother would become nervous and that would not be good for her health which was already very frail. He put Leonora down very gently and asked the servant who was with him to bring a bowl with hot water. He would have to clean her up before the doctor arrived.

Nestor tore her clothes away with care as he didn't want to scare her and cleaned her body delicately, removing the dirt, so the wounds wouldn't get infected. He was very careful not to cause her any undue pain. His worry was as clear as his love. Even if he was the best actor in the world, he wouldn't be able to play the role of an uncle. It was clear for whoever wanted to see: Nestor was madly in love with Leonora.

The doctor came quickly, as requested, and started immediately to check for broken bones. He applied treatments to the wounds and prescribed her medicine to be taken every hour. In case of fever, he told Nestor to place a compress on her forehead. If she didn't get any better, call him, he would come as soon as possible. Nestor made himself comfortable next to her and took her temperature constantly—besides giving her the medicine as prescribed. When Leonora became a little warm, he placed a cold compress on her forehead.

When Leonora woke up, she looked at him and held his hands. Her face was flushed from the fever. She had red lips and the look of someone who was in love. Still numbed by the effect of drugs, she soon returned to sleep.

"How I love you… how I want you… help me not to love you so much—teach me how to overcome

this love. God no! Help me, I cannot give in; I cannot cope any longer," thought Nestor.

In a short while, happy to see Nestor with a passionate look at her side, taking care of her, she felt safe, protected and overcome with fatigue, slept again.

The heat of her body burning with fever, her lips so close to his, everything was stronger than any promise, than any oath—Nestor was just someone in love. He didn't know where to find the strength to resist such love. He kissed her lips so tenderly, that Leonora could hardly recall what had happened.

Nestor stood up, and sat in an armchair next to Leonora. He stayed there during the whole night looking at the woman who made him forget that he was married. He could no longer deceive her—he would soon have to tell her of his marriage. As soon as her condition improved he would tell her why he had come back.

Once again, life was testing those involved in this drama of pain and love. Nestor should resist the love he felt for Leonora, and she should control her hate and understand that the love she had for Nestor as a woman could not be consummated in this life, given the thorny road which in a moment of supreme pain was chosen by her. In addition, the unfolding of all these events, unchained by extreme hate, caused many deaths.

The opposing force to good, invoked by Helen, went on to follow her, emanating evil at every opportunity—not allowing love to defeat hate in Leonora's heart. When each difficult situation presented itself, Leonora yielded to this weakness and committed herself increasingly to the laws of life. This was the objective of evil, to cause more and more pain and suffering.

Chapter 6 - The Search for Truth

Three weeks had passed since Leonora's accident. Her wounds were healing nicely and she was feeling much better. Her uncle did not leave her side for a second—he looked after her with all the care of a doting father. During her recovery time Leonora did not mention the love they felt for each other, nor force any situation which would leave Nestor embarrassed. She acted as his niece the whole time.

Elizabeth felt better, as if she knew the importance of helping Nestor at that moment, who was always very busy taking care of Leonora. Many letters had arrived from Paris; it was Rose, worried about his delay. Nestor received them, read them and kept them in his bedroom. He answered only two, telling her what had happened to Leonora and how she was still recovering, and needed care.

Many times Nestor asked Leonora what had happened on the day of the accident and where she had been. Her answer was always evasive; she said she had gone for a ride and had gotten lost—it was dark and she couldn't see properly. She thought a cat had run past the horse, which got spooked and threw her off.

And this was exactly what had happened. Her cat had gone after her that afternoon. She didn't notice she had been followed. Remembering now what had happened, Leonora was deeply intrigued by the cat's attitude, as she knew it would never do something against her.

"How could her cat do that to her, spook her horse and cause her fall?" thought Leonora.

Many times she had tried to call her cat, but Nestor was always around, so she didn't have the opportunity to look for it. Not being able to walk unaided made it very difficult to search for it. That afternoon, she started to walk without Nestor's help and was in the garden when the priest arrived.

"Good afternoon, Leonora, how have you been? Much better, I see."

"Much better indeed, father! Thanks to my uncle, who was tireless in looking after me."

"It's true. Where can I find him? I would like to talk to Nestor."

"Come in, I'll let him know you are here."

Leonora walked very calmly inside, asking the servant to let Nestor know of the visit.

"Good afternoon, father, what a pleasure to have you here. To what do I owe the pleasure of your visit?"

"Well, Nestor, what I came here to do, in truth, is to pay a visit to your mother, but when I learned of your return I decided to speak to your first."

"Of course, father, is there a problem? You seem to be a little worried."

Leonora was still near the two when the priest gave Nestor a discreet look and the latter asked:

"Is it private? I understand. Leonora my angel, leave us alone for a while. Go see your grandmother, but be very careful on the stairs. Well, father, let's talk in the office. Please, follow me. Would you like something to drink, some juice or tea?"

"No, thanks. I would like to ask what you think of a letter I have in my power."

"A letter? What do you mean?"

"Well, I'll tell you. The Inquisitor, before dying, gave me a mission. That I should deliver this letter to Madam Elizabeth, your mother."

"It's been so many years since he died and only now you mention this letter!"

"It's true, but so many things have happened since then, that I ended up forgetting I had the letter. I know I made a mistake, but when I remembered to bring it and told your mother that I would do so there was a new tragedy in your family; your sister's death which left your mother very poorly."

"But father, it's been so long, I don't understand what you are getting at."

"Calm down, my son, I will explain. I was the Inquisitor's roommate during many years—we always had long conversations. Once he confessed something I won't be able to reveal. It was a short time before his tragic death. I followed his suffering in life after the accident, heard his moaning and grunting in pain during the night, his nightmares and his remorse."

"Come on, father, say it quickly!"

"Well, as I was saying, I learnt what happened some years ago and that it really affected your lives. I know that in this letter the Inquisitor talks about this with your mother and because of her ill health, I am in doubt whether to hand in the letter."

Nestor kept on thinking about his words: *"Something that really affected your lives..."*

"Father, tell me what it concerns—what is written in this letter?"

"Child, I am not allowed to say, all I know was told to me in confession, I can't reveal it... and the letter is addressed to your mother, therefore, only she can open it."

"How will I know whether to hand it in to my mother or not?"

"That's exactly my doubt. What to do? I think she must have forgotten this letter, as we have never talked about this subject again; but at the same time my consciousness is demanding that I resolve this issue. I made a promise that I would hand it into Madam Elizabeth's hands."

Nestor spoke:

"Well, leave it in my possession. I will think about it carefully and decide what is better for her."

The priest was already leaving the office. Nestor looked at the letter, when he heard his question:

"What does Leonora have to do with this letter? You asked her to leave so we could talk, therefore, I must conclude that you did not wish for her to know the subject of our conversation."

"You concluded correctly. I think everything is linked to Leonora—I just don't know up to what point."

Then the priest proceeded to meet Elizabeth, leaving Nestor holding the letter and quite curious about its content. Leonora, who was keeping her grandmother company, was anxious to learn what they talked about in the office. The grandmother noticed her disquiet and tried to relieve her worries, by telling her that it was probably nothing of importance but a subject not befitting a woman. At this moment, they were interrupted by two light knocks on the door.

"You may come in," said Leonora.

"Make yourself at home, father—I'll leave the two of you alone."

Leonora left towards the office. She wanted to look at Nestor, to see if his expression showed any change. Her heart told her that her worries were founded. When she opened the door, she saw Nestor sitting down, with hands holding his head, looking at a letter which was on the desk.

"What happened, Uncle Nestor? You look troubled."

Nestor tried to disguise his feelings and hid the letter, thinking that Leonora hadn't seeing it.

"Nothing, my angel, the priest needs some help for his church, so he came to ask me for a financial donation."

She pretended to believe his words, but his reaction on hiding the letter, made Leonora certain he was concealing something really serious, and sooner or later she would attempt to discover what it was.

Meanwhile, Elizabeth asked the priest what he had talked about with Nestor, but, not knowing what to say, he tried to cover up by changing the subject. The priest's attitude made her worried.

"I see that you are healthier and healthier. Your son's arrival was a miraculous medicine for you. You can already talk—so I want to see when you leave the bed."

Speaking slowly and at her own pace, Elizabeth responded:

"I'm happy! Everybody is happy, we have some peace at last."

"I'll pray my friend, may your home remain in peace for a very long time."

They spent a few more minutes talking, till the priest said goodbye and left. He came down the stairs and went to meet Leonora and Nestor, to say goodbye to them as well. They walked him to the garden, saying:

"May God have mercy on us all."

"May God be with you, my children. I know you need His presence here."

Nestor thanked him and glanced at his niece who did not say anything, but only observed him. Her look was of curiosity, she knew what he was trying to say to the priest; it was related to the letter that Nestor tried to hide from her. After the priest left, Leonora turned to Nestor and said:

"Tell me uncle, why are you hiding from me the real motive of this visit?"

Nestor looked at her, somewhat shocked by her inconvenient question, and replied:

"I've already told you everything—I have no reason to hide anything from you."

Nestor's voice sounded as untrue as his words. Leonora did not appreciate his attitude. She started to get nervous, thinking that there was something wrong in their relationship and this upset her. She started to demonstrate again an emotional loss of control. Her eyes looked like they changed color and got bigger, her appearance had become heavier, which made her look even more like Helen.

Nestor observed her change and was increasingly disconcerted. How could this happen? He asked Leonora to remain calm, there was no reason for her to become nervous because the priest spoke to him without her being present. Leonora then asked:

"Why have you hidden the letter from me?"

"Which letter? I don't remember any letter."

"Stop, Uncle Nestor! You don't know how to lie, you never have, and you are not going to start now."

Nestor felt a bit embarrassed. He had never really lied; except about his marriage—a detail for which he still did not have the courage to tell her. He didn't know how to hide the truth from anyone, especially from Leonora.

"You're right, I didn't want to say anything because this is a matter that concerns only your grandmother. But I'll tell you."

He told her the whole conversation with the priest, omitting the part, of course, when he talked about Leonora.

"What happened in the past which has so influenced our lives? Which secret is this, Uncle Nestor, aren't you curious?"

Nestor started to wonder, listening to Leonora. His mind was elsewhere at that moment—he was afraid it was something from the past which he wouldn't like to relive ever again. To remember Helen was painful, even after so many years. He hadn't forgotten any detail of the tragic day of her death.

At this moment, the memory of Helen's eyes was imbedded in Nestor's mind—they showed so much hate that they were unforgettable. He noticed that Leonora, when having an emotional breakdown, clearly had the same eyes. Leonora interrupted his thoughts:

"Answer, uncle, wouldn't you like to find out the letter's content?"

"Yes, I would, but I can't. It is addressed to your grandmother. We can't open it. It would be an outrage to the social norms of good behavior."

"How will you know whether to hand it in or not?"

"I don't know, Leonora, I have to think. You are more curious than I am—but don't you dare to touch that letter, understand?"

"I wouldn't do it without with your permission, besides, I don't know where it is."

She gave a weak smile, looking like a child ready to be naughty.

Nestor was charmed by her behavior. They laughed together and talked a little in the garden. The rest of the day transpired easily, nothing else disturbed the monotony of that place.

Next morning Nestor woke up very early; he had gone to bed thinking about the past and decided to go back to the grotto. He had to pay a visit to the place. He had promised himself he would not go back, but the memories from the previous day made him forget his promise. Leonora heard his movement early in the morning and decided to get up and see what was happening.

"Good morning uncle, you are up early, are you going out?"

"Before anything else, can you tell me what you are doing up at this time in your nightgown downstairs? I've already told you are not a child any longer, you cannot walk around the house half naked in front of the servants."

"Goodness, that's excessive, Uncle Nestor. The old butler can no longer see much, you can rest assured, and at this time there isn't anyone else here."

"Yes, there is, me, your uncle, but I'm also a man. You need to show some modesty!"

"Uncle, you changed my diapers and are tired of seeing my body. Why do I need to be careful?"

"It has nothing to do with being careful but …"

Nestor interrupted what he was going to say and added:

"Leonora, you win, I am not going to talk about this again, but go change and come back to have breakfast with me."

Leonora came very close, to the point of touching Nestor's arm. This made him feel a tingling sensation over his whole body. The scent of her subtle perfume, her loose hair touching his face, inebriated him; he could see her breasts through her nightgown. He could hardly speak, so he got all his strength together and asked:

"Go get changed, Leonora, please."

"Very well, but wait until I come back so we can have breakfast together."

Nestor tried to recover: he was breathless; his heart was racing; he could hardly think.

"I need to pluck up the courage to tell them today—I can no longer hide this marriage. Leonora needs to know so she'll stop obsessing about me."

Nestor knew it wasn't going to be that easy once Leonora found out. He was afraid of her reaction. He didn't want to hurt her or make her suffer. He would have to find the right words, and be very calm. He thought about it quite a lot, but was still perplexed about the best way to tell her. Then, he asked Louiza for help; for her to enlighten him at such a difficult time. He was already in the dining room when Leonora came in. She was dressed for riding, which surprised Nestor greatly.

"Where do you think you are going, dressed like that?"

"I'm going riding—I want to go with you."

"No, you're not. You still haven't fully recovered and besides that I can't take you where I'm going."

Leonora tried to argue but to no avail. As she already knew where he was going, she did not pry any further. They had breakfast in silence. Nestor, who wanted to say something, looked at her, and exchanged glances.

"What is it, uncle, I feel you want to tell me something?"

"Could you ask my mother to join us for dinner tonight? I have an announcement to make to both of you."

"An announcement?"

"Yes! You'll find out at dinner."

"Alright, I'll inform grandmother, but we have to eat earlier, as she finds it hard to stay awake until very late."

"I understand. I'm going out now and will be back at sunset. I will not be here for lunch."

Leonora watched as Nestor left. As always, her sixth sense told her that something bad was about to happen. She started to feel anxious trying to imagine what it could be. During the day all she could do was pace up and down the hallways of the house—she couldn't concentrate on anything. Her demeanor had already changed—her face had turned heavy and she simply wasn't the same anymore. She went in and out of Elizabeth's room many times; her grandmother could tell dinner was going to be tragic.

After her granddaughter gave to Elizabeth the message, she was certain that Nestor's news wouldn't be good for Leonora. She just couldn't imagine how bad it was going to be for everyone. She then started to pray and ask for help from all the saints—she could tell that peace was about to end.

Leonora was in her room, walking around aimlessly. She was very nervous. She knew her emotional balance was hanging by a thread and did not want to remain in such a state. She remembered her guardian angel and began to call him.

"Bartholomew, I need you… I don't seem to be able to calm down… I can feel the hate in my heart, please, come help me."

There was a beam of light, as if suddenly many candles had been lit. Leonora looked for Bartholomew. When she turned around, she saw Louiza. She was so shocked she screamed:

"Aunt Louiza, is that you?"

With her calm and gentle voice, Louiza answered:

"My dear daughter, calm down, I'm here to help you."

Leonora cried, overcome with emotion. She wanted to hug Louiza, but she couldn't move.

"Leonora, feel the love in your heart now. Remember that those who were to blame have already paid for their crimes. Learn how to forgive. Nestor loves you very much, but you have also made many mistakes and will have to pay for them. Believe what he says, listen with your heart and don't let yourself be guided by so much hate. Everything has already gone past, and in a new life you'll have the opportunity to learn through resignation and love to reconcile with the people involved in the difficult moments in your present life."

"I don't understand what you mean, aunt!"

"You will understand. The important thing is to remember my words at the right moment. Have faith in the Creator, know that in this life you came to look for revenge and not to forgive. This was your biggest mistake. Be yourself and listen to your heart."

Having said that, Louiza's spirit disintegrated like smoke, leaving Leonora in floods of tears. Overcome by tiredness, she went to bed and slept during which time her spirit went to Bartholomew, in the grotto.

"You came to me. You managed to cleanse your heart from hate—this is a big victory for us."

"I'm not sure I have managed, but I need your help. I'm aware you know everything about what has been happening—including that I also was with aunt Louiza and I couldn't quite understand what she meant."

"Leonora, we have talked a lot about reincarnation and your aunt tried to talk to you exactly about that: of your past life, your death and how you swore vengeance. You invoked some force of evil and it has been with you since your death and reincarnation as Leonora. You need to destroy it and only you can do it."

"But how? I don't even know where this evil force you talk about is."

"You'll destroy it with love in your heart which will destroy the hate you feel for your family. You will find out where this force comes from."

Leonora gave a deep sigh, waking up immediately. After Bartholomew's words, she had calmed down, but still had a heart burdened with sorrow. She went to check whether Nestor had already arrived. As he hadn't, she went to Elizabeth's bedroom; she was sleeping.

Reminding herself of the words she heard in her dreams, Leonora kept looking at Elizabeth, not able to understand how she could feel so much hatred towards this little old lady who slept like an angel. She thought of her mother, Isabel, so defenseless in her wheel chair and who had done nothing to her; of her grandfather, who in spite of being so young, she could remember in detail his suffering and the lack of pity she felt towards him; and her fond memories of Louiza, who had been a real mother and had saved her from being an orphan.

Everything went through her mind in a matter of seconds, while she observed Elizabeth. She went to her bedroom to await Nestor. When she went in, her cat was scratching the window glass, asking to get in.

"Aha! So you've decided to come back, cheeky—she opened the window to let her cat in—how could you do that to me, did you think I'd forget? You crossed the road in front of my horse only for it to throw me off. Aren't you my friend anymore?"

She stared at her cat for a few seconds, and through its eyes the cat answered her question. Suddenly aware of what was happening she was a little frightened, she could not understand how she was able to read her pet's thoughts.

"Have I understood you correctly? Are you trying to tell me that you only did that to bring me closer to Nestor? I must be out of my mind thinking that a cat is answering my questions… but still, if this was your intention, I'm grateful. I have finally found someone who is prepared to help me with Nestor."

The cat made itself comfortable on her lap and Leonora went on stroking its fur, and thinking aloud.

"I can't wait to see him, I'm so anxious about what he's going to say. I'd love to know what this dinner is about."

Meowing, the cat jumped off her lap, moving towards the door.

"What is it? Would you like to leave?"

Leonora stood up and opened the door. The cat left the room and started to meow as if it were calling her. Leonora understood what it wanted and followed it, stopping in front of Nestor's room.

"You want me to go in, right?"

Another meow. She opened the door, and followed the cat who went straight to the desk, and tried to open the drawer but it was locked. Leonora moved closer and tried to open it. Without any success, she started to look for the key.

"It isn't here, it must be with Uncle Nestor. There's something here I should see, is that it?"

Another meow.

"Come on, let's leave as Uncle Nestor should be arriving soon. I'll find a way to get the key without him noticing it."

As she heard Nestor's voice coming from the main door she ran, got the cat and placed it outside. She came back and walked in Nestor's direction. She noticed his eyes were sad and bitter.

"What happened, you look very sad—didn't your outing go as you planned?"

"It's nothing. Is everything ok here?"

"Yes, I've already told grandmother that dinner will be served earlier and that you have asked her to be present."

"All right, Leonora. I'm going to have a bath and rest a little. Please call me half an hour before dinner, in case I'm still asleep."

"I will—have a rest and I'll wake you up."

Nestor climbed the stairs with his head low, as if he carried the weight of the world. He didn't even know how sad he was with the news he was about to deliver. Leonora, who knew everything about his feelings, thought:

"It must be very serious what Uncle Nestor has to say, I can feel his sadness. I need to find out where this key is."

Leonora wondered how she would manage to get it without being noticed. She waited for Nestor to have his bath in order to enter his bedroom and look for his clothes. Once there, she noticed that he got undressed in the bathroom. Annoyed, she realized she would have to wait until he fell asleep. Only that way would she have access to his clothes.

She waited patiently until Nestor fell asleep. Very quietly she reached for the pocket of his trousers, which were on the armchair. Carefully in order not to make any noise, she looked for the keys until she found it. She gently walked to the desk and opened the drawer slowly. There were many letters. Leonora didn't know what to look for so she looked one by one, until she saw an envelope sent by Rose. She took it and left quietly towards her bedroom—her heart beating fast. She was scared of opening the letter, but she had to do it. She decided to end her anguish, so she opened the letter and began to read what was written:

"Darling Nestor, I am very worried by your delay and am really missing you. I know that if you haven't come back yet, it's because you haven't managed to solve all the problems that took you back home. But, darling, come back as soon as possible—I have great news for you. Send my regards to your mother and Leonora, tell them that I am expecting them here in Paris. Send me news, I am anxious to know if you have already told everybody that we got married and how Elizabeth and especially Leonora reacted."

Unable to carry on reading, Leonora had a twisting pain in her heart—such was the blow from knowing that Nestor had gotten married. She wanted to scream, to do something to diminish her pain. She was deeply upset. She walked like an insane woman through the hallway towards Nestor's bedroom. She opened the door so loudly that he woke up shocked, not knowing what had happened.

"What's the meaning of this? Why do you enter my room like that?"

When he saw Leonora standing at the end of his bed, he almost let out a cry, it was Helen herself who was there.

"God, Helen, is that you?"

"No, Uncle Nestor, I'm Leonora! Not this Helen."

Leonora's voice shook with rage, like her body. Her eyes were pure hate and her nostrils opened and closed with such a speed that they seemed to release all her poison through them. Nestor couldn't say anything—all he could do was to look at that woman. He sat in wonder—he wanted to hug her, in spite of knowing he was before a vision.

"This is the second time you betrayed me— you've never loved me. How could you do this to me? I know now that you've always been a coward. How could I have loved you? How did I not see that you would betray me again?"

"For goodness sake, what are you saying?"

"That I hate you and your whole family. You are like everybody else and are as guilty as your mother."

"Guilty of what? I don't know what you are blaming me for! Leonora, please listen."

"No," she screamed.

"I'll never listen to you again; I'll never love you again."

Leonora was screaming so loud that the whole household could hear—but they couldn't understand all the noise that came from the bedroom. Elizabeth called for Nestor and she screamed for someone to come help her. She wanted to get up, to go to his bedroom and see what was happening. The servants did not dare to go upstairs. They were frightened by Leonora's screams. Elizabeth continued to scream for Leonora and Nestor. She tried to drag herself out of her bed. She fell on the floor and with a lot of effort she arrived at the door. She begged God to help her—she needed to get to Nestor's bedroom. She knew something bad was about to happen. At this exact moment, the cat entered the room. Elizabeth on seeing it demanded:

"Go away, you devil! You have done all this! You are responsible for all the disgrace in my family."

The cat bared its sharp claws and teeth and, very cleverly moved to where the burning candle was and dropped it on her bed. Everything caught on fire. There was a lot of smoke and the fire spread quickly throughout the bedroom. Elizabeth screamed for help, her clothes were on fire.

Meanwhile, Leonora screamed and hit Nestor as hard as she could. He tried to contain her, but it was almost impossible: her anger was such that she had the strength of two men. As they fought he called her name in order to calm her down, until he managed to make her still for a few seconds.

"Leonora, please listen my love, I love you very much, please believe me. I've done all this so you wouldn't get hurt. Our love is impossible, I treated you almost as a father … we cannot be lovers or …"

He was interrupted by Leonora's tears. She was so upset and cried so much that she could hardly utter a single word.

"Please don't cry, my love, I only want what is good for you."

When everything seemed to have calmed down, a horrifying cry came from Elizabeth's room. Nestor let go of Leonora and went to check on his mother. Even with the door closed he could see the room was on fire and shouted:

"Help! Bring buckets of water, my mother's room is on fire!"

Nestor opened the door, a blaze nearly reached him. Leonora was standing still in the hallway and when she saw what was happening, she started to cry and left running, she was terrified of fire. The scene of Leonora's death in her previous life was etched in her memory. She was reliving everything and could feel her body burning. Without control of her actions, she headed straight to some water, as if it were her body which was in flames.

Nestor threw a blanket over his mother's body which was engulfed in flames. He managed to remove her from the inferno, while the servants tried to extinguish the fire which still burnt in the room.

"My God! My mother!" Nestor cried, holding on to her body.

Elizabeth, as she laid there with her last breath of life looked at him and asked for forgiveness. When everything calmed down and the fire was out, the servants came close to Nestor and tried to soothe him, so he might be able to decide what to do next. That was when Nestor sent for the priest to come and pray for his mother's soul.

The funeral was then arranged. Nestor sent a letter to his brother informing him of the sad tragedy involving their mother. Then, he looked for Leonora, but couldn't find her, nobody saw her after the fire in Elizabeth's room. He couldn't be absent during the burial but he was very worried and concerned about Leonora's disappearance.

Meanwhile, Leonora had run to the river and dived in to feel her skin wet, as she had the sensation her whole body had burned.

After that, not knowing which way to take, as Leonora felt totally lost she walked, despite intense leg pain, all the way to the grotto. She was very tired, since the place was a good distance from her home. It was becoming dark. She was in a regrettable state, one felt pity just by looking at her, for this was what Leonora looked like, a lost child, completely alone in the world, as if she carried a very heavy load and could not carry it any more.

Leonora cried a lot as she approached the grotto entrance. It was very dark, but she was so sad that she didn't even notice it. Once entered, she walked towards the stone altar, laid down and there she stayed, curled up and in silence. She didn't want to think, didn't want to remember anything that had happened, all she wanted was to be in silence, nothing else.

The day was breaking, Leonora was still motionless. She looked into space as if she was in a state of shock, until she heard a very familiar voice.

"Leonora don't be like that. You need to react, to go back home, to go to your grandmother's funeral."

"I won't—she said quietly—I don't want to see her. I don't want to see anyone from that family."

Bartholomew calmly said:

"You mustn't run away now for you still have to fulfill your karma—don't let hate take you over. Go and forgive Elizabeth, before it is too late."

"I can't," she said crying.

"Yes, you can, Leonora, you are stronger than you think. Elizabeth's body is still there, go and forgive her whole-heartedly."

"Bartholomew, it wasn't I who killed my grandmother, was it?! Tell me!"

"My dear, every time you feel hate, you release the force of evil towards all that you hate, and through this force you fulfill your revenge."

"Does it mean I've killed my grandmother?"

"In a way yes, and no. I've already told you: there is this evil's force that follows you, that needs to be destroyed."

"I loved my grandmother. I didn't want it to happen. At the time, when her bedroom caught on fire, I was fighting with Nestor. At that moment, I was so angry and full of hate in my heart, that I didn't realize what had caused the fire."

Then, Leonora started to cry—tears rolled down her face while she talked.

"I don't know how it happens. I just know that at times when I'm angry the bad thought comes, and I'm not able to control it, and I wish that everybody suffers the same way I do."

"Don't waste anymore time, Leonora, go back and forgive Elizabeth. Only in this way will you be able to win this battle. Don't forget that the only way to beat the force of evil is through love."

Leonora left the grotto and ran as fast as she could. After a while, she was exhausted, out of breath, but she had to arrive on time. They could not bury Elizabeth without her being present. As she ran she prayed, without realizing it. She asked God to give her the strength to continue; her heart was in agony with the possibility of not arriving on time. She asked God to help her, to do something, even a miracle, but not let her grandmother be buried without her being there.

Everybody was already leaving the chapel and carrying the coffin when they saw Leonora running down the road. She looked a bit crazy and screamed for them to wait for her. Nestor was very surprised and relieved. Her appearance, though, left everybody present a somewhat frightened. Her clothes were all torn and dirty; her hair was all tangled up as if it hadn't been combed for a long time and her face was swollen from so much crying. She threw herself over the coffin, and cried incessantly. She asked for forgiveness. The scene was very touching, all could feel Leonora's pain.

"Elizabeth, forgive me. I've always loved you. Please forgive me, grandmother…"

Nestor tried to comfort her; but she didn't even look at him, let alone answer him. She was stuck to the coffin, howling. While they witnessed the suffering, they didn't realize that the priest was behind her praying, asking God to help that child. He knew what was happening to Leonora. Although he was a priest, he had always read spiritual books—which were actually forbidden—and was very sensitive. He could feel the presence of Isabel and Louiza's spirits getting close to Leonora. As they stroked her hair Louiza said:

"My darling! Elizabeth has already forgiven you, no need to despair. What is necessary is for you to forgive her! What she needs is your forgiveness, for her soul to find peace!"

Leonora looked around to see where her aunt's voice was coming from when the priest turned around and said:

"She's right next to you, Leonora!"

She looked at the priest and couldn't understand how he knew what she was looking for. She thought:

"He's a priest—can he see spirits as well?"

As if he read her mind, Father Gabriel spoke for just her to hear:

"Leonora, although I belong to the Catholic Church, I know a lot about spirits. I've read many books that belonged to the village's priest—he had a collection on the theme of spirituality."

So, Father Gabriel moved Leonora away from the coffin, and tenderly said:

"Let's continue with the burial—on any of these days we'll talk about this subject."

Nestor was very intrigued by this conversation for Leonora never liked priests. She didn't give them even a minute of her time. No one was ever able to talk to her before. But Father Gabriel was able to, even in a moment of so much suffering.

"Go home now my child. As your aunt said, your grandmother has already forgiven you."

Not saying a word, Leonora lowered her head and walked towards the house. She didn't look at anyone, not even Nestor—she acted as if he wasn't there.

Divine providence had put to test the characters in this plot of love and hate. After so much suffering, Leonora managed to forgive, from the bottom of her heart, her biggest tormentor, Elizabeth. Leonora was completely destroyed by the pain and sadness she felt due to her grandmother's death.

Elizabeth had died the same way she had caused Helen's death; thus re-balancing part of the negative karma she had accumulated in this life. She learnt a lot through her suffering, culminating in the extreme pain of her last moments.

Nestor's greatest dilemma now, was how to tell Leonora that he should look after her. He had to do it confined to the role of a father, although he loved her as a man, without causing her any more pain. It was necessary to make her understand that this was the right path to follow in this life.

Chapter 7 - Painful Discoveries

Two weeks had passed. Leonora was ill, or rather emotionally disturbed and acted as if she were very distressed. Nestor didn't know what to do. Since the day of Elizabeth's death, she hadn't said a word. She spent her time looking at the walls, refusing to eat. It took Nestor a lot of effort to make her take some soup.

Nestor was tireless, he spent hours in her company trying to talk, but in vain—she didn't even look at him. He was so desperate that he asked Father Gabriel to come and talk to her.

Nestor wrote a letter to his wife describing Leonora's psychological state. He said he wouldn't return to Paris until Leonora was better and asked why his brother Sebastian hadn't come to their mother's seventh day mass.

Immediately after the burial, Nestor had received a letter from Rose, talking about her feelings in regards to everything that had happened, but that her state of health was delicate and she'd like to tell him about it personally. She'd wait for his reply—she wanted to know whether there would be any difficulty if she came to see him.

Nestor didn't know what to say; he wanted to know what the problem with Rose was, but he feared Leonora. The thought of having both together, his heart warned him, wasn't a good idea. He was in the garden writing a response letter to Rose when Father Gabriel arrived.

"Good morning Father Gabriel, I'm so glad you could come. I really need your help. I don't know what else to do with Leonora, she's still very disturbed."

After telling him what had happened, he asked:

"Can you help me?"

"I believe so, I'll try. But before I see her, I'd like you to tell me what you did with the letter from the Inquisitor that I gave to you"

Nestor had forgotten the letter.

"It's in my room—I didn't have time to tell my mother about it."

"Keep it that way, my son. Every time I tried to hand it to your mother a tragedy would befall this house. It seems the same thing happened to you. I don't know why, but it's as if it were cursed. I know I shouldn't pay too much attention to this sort of thing, but there were too many coincidences for me to ignore it. I beg you, don't touch it for now."

"All right, father, but please go see Leonora. See if she says something. I know she doesn't really like priests, never has, maybe it'll be different with you. Since the burial, the only person she spoke to, surprisingly, has been you."

"Don't worry, Nestor, I'll try."

On saying that, Father Gabriel walked to Leonora's room. When he went past Elizabeth's room he gave a long sigh and prayed. He felt her presence in the house and thought:

"There still is something worrying this soul— she's still heavily afflicted."

He made the sign of the cross and went ahead.

He knocked on Leonora's door and nothing, no sign of life. He opened it very slowly and looked for her inside. There was no one on her bed, so he opened the door a little more and went in. When he saw Leonora sitting down, all curled up on the corner, she looked like a subdued animal.

"My child, what are you doing sitting down like that? Come here."

Father Gabriel took Leonora's hands and guided her to her bed, sat down next to her and said:

"Leonora, you need to react, this attitude won't help you. You need to talk, tell me how you're feeling. What are you afraid of?"

"Fire… I don't want to die in a fire. I'm scared of my grandmother!"

"Scared of your grandmother, but why? Do you think she's coming back to get you, is that it?"

"I don't know, but since the day of my grandmother's death I've been dreaming about burning—that everybody's laughing while I suffer in pain."

Father Gabriel understood what was happening to Leonora. After the shock of the accident, she had flashes of her past life, or rather she relived everything, not conscious to the fact that she was having a regression. He didn't know how to explain what had happened, but he had an idea:

"Leonora, there are some books which belonged to Father Bartholomew and I wish…"

When he said that name, Leonora looked at him. She was very surprised, and said:

"Father Bartholomew! Do you mean you know my guardian angel, or rather, Brother Bartholomew?"

Father Gabriel, startled by Leonora's revelation, said:

"I never met him. I wasn't here at the time he passed away, many years ago; but when they sent me to this village I was at his chapel for some time and discovered hidden among his belongings a collection of books on spirits."

"So that's why I never found them."

"What do you mean—did you know about their existence?"

"I'll tell you everything so that you can better understand this story. When Bartholomew sent me looking for such books I went to the chapel and could not find anything—however I didn't know he was a priest!"

They talked for hours. Nestor was astonished at Leonora's change in regards to the priest. He couldn't ever imagine her talking for so long to one of them.

Gabriel was really emotional with Leonora's account. He believed in spirits—at the funeral he felt their presence, but had never heard anything like Leonora's story. He looked at that child, for Leonora still looked like a child, not knowing what to say. He was certain she had paranormal powers. He didn't believe in witches, as before, in spite of the fact that some priests still believed they really existed.

Gabriel was a very different priest. He had a broader vision of what religion is, he'd read many books on all of them, many of them actually forbidden by the church, which made him change his way of thinking and acting compared to his contemporaries. Very few priests knew about his expansive knowledge—the majority only knew he was in demand for solving cases of possession.

"Leonora, my child, I'll bring you Father Bartholomew's books. I think they'll help you understand everything that's been happening to you. And who knows, to Nestor too, as he's really suffering with everything that's going on."

On hearing his name, Leonora went stiff. Gabriel noticed the change and asked her:

"What's the matter? Why did you react that way when I mentioned Nestor's name?"

"I don't want to talk about him father. Don't mention his name anymore—he's dead to me."

"Nonsense, my child, you know very well he adores you and is very worried about your state of health."

"I don't want to know father—please be quiet!"

Father Gabriel didn't insist. Then, he said goodbye and promised to come back as soon as he could to bring the books for Leonora. Returning to the garden, he spoke to Nestor.

"Be very patient with your niece, she's feeling very upset with you. She didn't tell me why, but she didn't even want to hear your name."

"I'll tell you what happened. It'll be easier for you to help us. I feel I can trust you. I wouldn't want this story to become town gossip. I don't need to ask you for confidentiality."

"You can rest assured, my child, it'll be a confession."

Thus Nestor told the priest the whole story, from Helen's death to Leonora's birth, their physical resemblance, her emotional change when she became nervous, and her behavioral changes.

Nestor took a deep breath and continued to speak about the love they felt for each other; told him about his sister's death and his promise, and finally, of his secret marriage that Leonora had found out.

So, Father Gabriel started to put the puzzle together. Now all the mystery was becoming clearer, he could understand better and link the facts, spiritually talking.

"Nestor, I'm bringing Leonora some books about spirits. I'd like you to read them as well—that way I'll be able to help you both."

"Books about spirits? I don't understand, you're a priest—how is it possible?"

"Priests also believe in spirits and especially in life after death, my child. But I beg you: keep this a secret, as there are many priests who still don't believe in it and if they knew of my conviction, they would cause me serious problems."

"Don't worry father, I'll never talk to anyone about this."

"I'm leaving now. I have a lot to do at the church. God be with you—I'll come back as quickly as I can."

Gabriel left Nestor alone with his thoughts. He kept looking for a few minutes in the direction of Leonora's bedroom window; he would love to talk to her, to explain everything, to make her understand and, who knows, perhaps she would forgive him.

Next morning, Leonora got up very early. She was feeling better so she thought of going for a walk. Her intention was to go to the grotto, but she wasn't sure she would be strong enough to go that far.

She got up and left the room—when she went past Elizabeth's room she stopped and stared at it: the door was closed. She broke into a cold sweat only from looking at the signs of fire on the door, but she still decided to open it.

Feeling anguish in her chest, Leonora entered looking at the rest of the ashes in the room, when she saw everything burned, she started to feel sick, as if reliving her death again.

At this moment, she could see fire at every corner, and started to feel suffocated, she wanted to leave but she couldn't, something was holding her back. Maybe it was the fear, the terror of fire.

Without realizing what was happening Leonora started to scream, she couldn't control herself, she felt like her body was in flames, and unable to endure all the emotion of the moment, she fainted.

Nestor got up when he heard the screams and left his room desperate to check on what was happening. He ran in the direction of Leonora's room, but she wasn't there. He then proceeded to call her.

"Leonora, where are you?"

When he saw the door of Elizabeth's room open, he ran and found her unconscious on the floor.

"My love, what are you doing here?"

Nestor took Leonora into his arms and carried her to her room. He patted her face gently, trying to wake her up.

"Leonora, my angel, talk to me! Come on, wake up, everything's ok now."

"The fire, where's the fire?"

Leonora cried and between the tears she mumbled:

"I'm burnt. It hurts."

"Calm down, my darling, it was only a nightmare—there isn't any fire here and you aren't burnt."

Only then did Leonora realize where she was and who she was with. Carried away by emotion, she threw herself into Nestor's arms, and in tears she said repeatedly:

"Don't abandon me. Don't leave me alone. I'll die if you leave. They're going to kill me—I know!"

"Who is going to kill you Leonora, what are you saying? I won't leave you—I'll take you with me."

"Take me to where, Uncle Nestor? I don't want to go anywhere—I want to stay here with you."

"Let's not talk about this now, my angel—please, stop crying—you've had enough excitement. You need to become stronger and healthier—then we'll talk about what we're going to do with our lives."

"Uncle Nestor, stay with me, don't leave me, I don't want to be left alone."

"All right, I'll spend the whole day by your side. We'll take our time talking, but for now I'll order your breakfast, with lots of fruit and a good glass of milk."

Nestor wiped her tears and kissed her gently. At that moment, his desire was to grab her, kiss her all over and not let her go. He had to really restrain himself not to give in to his desire. He couldn't understand how he actually managed to resist this urge, as what he felt was so strong—not even he knew he could love a child so much, in such a way—a child who was like a daughter to him.

Leonora and Nestor had breakfast together in the bedroom and hardly talked. She couldn't take her eyes off him—which made him feel uncomfortable. She looked at Nestor with intensity as if trying to hypnotize him, sometimes by a look of tenderness, sometimes by bitterness.

In fact, Leonora's eyes were a great mystery to Nestor. There were moments when Nestor stopped breathing, or at least that's what it felt like to him, such was the strength of her gaze. Leonora's eyes seemed to talk to him, giving orders. He tried to avoid them, but it was in vain: they were stronger than him. When her appearance changed giving Leonora the likeness of another person, it was impossible for Nestor to think rationally.

At that moment, it was exactly what took place: Nestor got up, and as if Leonora's eyes were in command of his legs and of his will he walked in her direction, with his heart pounding hard. He knew what he was about to do, but couldn't stop. With their eyes locked together, he leaned, falling on top of her, when she whispered:

"Come, my love. I can't resist anymore… I need you and want you all for myself."

Nestor was in an uncontrolled state of passion. He kissed her so intensely that Leonora could hardly breathe. He moaned and talked at the same time.

"I can't. I mustn't."

Still, Nestor continued to kiss her. Gently, he lowered the strap of her nightdress, leaving her breasts exposed. On seeing them Nestor felt his desire becoming stronger, he seemed to be another man, he kissed her breasts, her neck. He completely lost his mind. He tore her clothes furiously, more like an animal in heat. Leonora wasn't the least scared—it was as if she were in command, always whispering:

"Come Nestor, love me, I'm all yours. Come my love, take me."

Every time Leonora made moaning sounds in his ears, Nestor went wild with desire. When everything seemed lost, that Nestor was going to take Leonora, something happened. A strong gust of wind entered the room, throwing everything on the floor. That was when Nestor noticed the presence of a black cat on the window sill. As the wind blew, the window caught its tail, and made it meow in pain, and that in turn brought them out of their trance.

"Oh Lord, had it not been for the wind catching this cat's tail…"

Nestor was bewildered. He looked at Leonora, naked on her bed; he could remember everything but couldn't understand how it got to that point. It was too close to being too late.

Leonora looked as if she were in shock—her face was blushing from emotion. On realizing that she was naked, she tried to cover herself up, as she was embarrassed by the way he looked at her body. Nestor moved away from the bed, shaking his head; he didn't know what to say. He sat down in front of her and said:

"Forgive me Leonora, it was stronger than me."

"I know, Uncle Nestor, it was stronger than me as well."

"Do you understand now why I had to marry Rose? What we feel for each other is not normal, it cannot be materialized, this force that takes over us, this passion that won't let us reason, this is all crazy! I raised you as a daughter. I should never have these feelings."

"Uncle Nestor, this is love, this force is called love!"

"No, Leonora, when you look like my girl I don't feel this. It is only when you transform yourself that you remind me of the woman who I most loved in this life, and that is exactly when I lose self-control. I don't love Leonora. I love Helen. Everything seems crazy, but it's true, you become like her, to the point of taking away my sanity, and that's wrong. Helen's dead and I need to remember that—I cannot believe you are her. Do you understand? Can you see why we cannot be together? I need to exorcise Helen's ghost who's inside me."

"If you need me to be this Helen in order to love me—then so be it!"

"Don't be silly, you don't know what you're saying!"

"Maybe her ghost is not inside you but inside me!"

Nestor thought about what Leonora just said. He had really thought about this possibility, but how could this happen? He did not understand anything about spirits, and did not believe in ghosts, but he felt something supernatural happened to Leonora. He then remembered the presence of the cat.

"The cat, where is it? It was on the window when the wind blew."

"It went away as soon as it got hurt. Don't be angry with it. It's only a harmless little cat."

"Leonora, does this cat belong to you?"

"Yes, Uncle Nestor, for a long time, I've always kept it because I know people don't like cats in this house."

"How did you find it?"

"I don't know, it appeared here in my bedroom when I was still very little."

"Then is it the same one who was here when your grandfather died?"

"I believe so, I don't remember, I was very young."

Nestor was left with a strange feeling about that cat. He was upset to learn of its presence in the house for so many years.

"Leonora, I don't want to see it inside the house again—please take it outside!"

"Ok, Uncle Nestor, don't be mad, I won't let it in again. Now tell me, when did you marry Rose?"

"It was a year ago—she really helped me at the time. After your aunt's death, I felt very lost in regards to my feelings, and everything I had promised her. I had to move away from here, because I couldn't forget you."

"Then it's true that you love me."

"No, stop Leonora, I've already explained what happened to me in relation to you. As I was saying, Rose feeling I wouldn't be strong enough to stay away from you suggested marriage. She loved me enough for the two of us and she convinced me that, with time, I would love her and forget you."

"What a stupid woman! You'll never forget me!"

"Don't talk like that about her, she's a good woman, gentle and sweet, and worries a lot about you."

"It's a lie, we hardly know each other and I've never liked her. Don't try to convince me that she's a wonderful woman, because you won't!"

"Leonora, she was really good to me. If you like me so much as you say, you must like her too."

"Do you love her Uncle Nestor?"

Nestor lowered his head; he didn't want to look into her eyes when answering that question. He knew Leonora would be able to read his eyes—that if he said yes he would be lying.

"Yes, I love her!"

"I don't believe you! It's a lie!"

"Calm down Leonora, please, enough of strong emotions for today—calm down!"

Leonora put her head on her pillow. She didn't want to talk anymore. To not feel any hate. Today she didn't have any strength to do anything, she wanted to be alone. She asked Nestor to leave, they would talk later on—she wanted to think.

Nestor obliged, asking her not to leave the room and if she needed anything to call for him, he'd be nearby.

Leonora was considering the latest events, when she saw in her mind the image of Nestor kissing and hugging her with all the passion a human being can feel. She didn't want that moment to ever end. She remembered his words, that he didn't love Leonora but Helen.

At this moment a heat came to her face, she didn't know whether it was anger or jealousy of her ghostly rival. But she couldn't hate Helen like she hated Rose or any other person who tried to keep them apart. Now, she had to find out who this woman was— how she had died. Nobody ever talked about what had happened to her, why her death had so shaken Nestor. It was a family secret and nobody talked about it under any circumstance. Nestor didn't even speak her name, and only today managed to talk to Leonora about Helen.

She stayed in bed for a long time, until, without realizing it, she fell asleep, worn out, overcame by so many emotions. She dreamed about her village: everybody was in the public square waiting anxiously for something to happen. Leonora was in the middle of the crowd asking what they were waiting for, and someone answered that the Inquisitor was going to burn someone at the stake.

"She's a witch, don't you know who she is?"

Leonora answered she didn't know who she was and asked:

"But why kill her? Has she ever done anyone any harm?"

"They said she didn't, but that her cat had—it operated with the devil."

Leonora looked at those people as if she recognized them from somewhere, until in the middle of the crowd she saw a familiar face, Father Bartholomew. Leonora ran to him, she wanted to talk to him, ask him what he was doing there and why he'd let that poor woman die in such a terrible way. However, as she tried to approach him he moved away. She couldn't reach him, even if he didn't appear to move.

Then there was a great silence in the square and Leonora heard a voice which she could never forget—the Inquisitor's voice. She turned around, looking in his direction. That was when she saw a woman tied to a piece of wood, the fire burning her entire body. She came closer—she couldn't believe what she was seeing. It was her.

At this moment, still asleep she yelled:

"It's me!" she cried. "You are burning me alive, it's me, Leonora. I'm not a witch!"

Still feeling overwhelmed by emotion, Leonora, with a cold sweat and tossing, woke up screaming:

"Take me away from here! I'm not a witch, don't kill me!"

Nestor entered Leonora's room, and found her completely distraught. She was deathly frightened from the dream and that scene. He didn't know what to do.

"Stop screaming, everything's all right. Come on, Leonora, wake up, they are not burning you."

Nestor gently slapped Leonora's face to wake her up. Even with her eyes opened, he knew she wasn't there, for some reason he couldn't understand, this wasn't Leonora. When he managed to calm her down she looked at him with so much pain in her eyes, that he hugged her, trying to comfort her, so she would stop shaking. And so nuzzled next to him, Leonora said:

"Uncle Nestor, I really need help, something bad is happening to me. We need to talk to the priest; he must have an answer for all this."

"But tell me, what happened."

"It was a dream, but it was so real, so real that I felt my body burning, being consumed by the fire."

"What fire? You're only shaken by what happened to your grandmother, that's all."

"That's not it, I'll tell you how it was, pay attention."

Then, Leonora tried to tell Nestor everything in detail. He listened to her and turned pale as she told her dream. He felt bad and left Leonora. He was upset; it was as if he had relived the whole tragic scene—his beloved Helen, burnt, dying and swearing vengeance.

"What is it uncle, are you upset about what I told you?"

"A little my love, but be calm. I'll send for the priest, he'll be able to give us an explanation for everything."

Nestor went downstairs and called a servant, giving him instructions to go ask the priest to come to the house as soon as he can. That he should come for dinner, if possible. He'd send the carriage to pick him up.

He waited in the garden for the servant's return with the answer and thought about everything that had happened. His head felt as if it were going to explode. He was sure that Leonora was possessed by Helen, he had no explanation for this phenomenon, but he knew that deep down this was the truth.

With so many things happening, Nestor forgot about Rose's last letter, which talked about the trip that Sebastian, her sister and herself would be taking the following week. Worried, he thought that this isn't the right moment for all of them to come, he was afraid of what might happen.

Then Nestor decided that he would write a letter to Rose, asking her to wait a little longer. He would let them know the best moment for them to come. He was heading to the office, when the servant arrived, bringing the priest's answer.

"Master, the priest asked me to tell you that he accepts the dinner invitation and that, please arrange transport for him when it's time."

"Great, tell the kitchen staff we have company for dinner."

Nestor headed to the office to write. He tried to explain as much as possible, so that Rose would be patient and wait for the next letter—and not come to visit now. When he finished the letter, he asked the servants to send it to Paris urgently and to let Leonora know about the dinner guest and for her to rest until then. He went to do the same.

The sun was already hiding behind the hills when Nestor woke up. He had a deep sleep. He had become exhausted with everything that had happened. As soon as he awoke he went downstairs to call the servant, asking him to send for a carriage to fetch the priest while he got ready.

One hour later Nestor was already waiting for his guest in the living room, having a good glass of wine, when Leonora appeared. She was wearing a beautiful sky blue dress. Her hair shone around her face, her mild perfume took over the room, leaving Nestor once again drunk from her presence. He could hardly look into her eyes—fearing her reaction.

"Would you like some wine?"

"Yes, I would. Who is coming for dinner, uncle?"

"The priest, darling. I've invited him, so we can talk."

"Good. I think he can help us."

"Do you really believe you need a priest's help, Leonora?"

"He's different from all the others. We've already talked and I'm not afraid of him."

"That's true, I've also found Father Gabriel to be different from the other priests we know."

They heard the sound of horses and went to the door to welcome the priest. To their great surprise it wasn't the carriage that had been sent to bring him. They waited to see who it was—a visitor at this hour? Nestor went pale when he saw his brother and his family. Rose followed behind. He looked at Leonora and her face was completely changed and her breathing accelerated.

"Calm down, Leonora, don't be like that, I didn't know they were coming today. I even wrote to them asking them not to come now, but they must have left before my letter arrived."

Leonora did not answer.

"Surprise!" said Sebastian.

"Brother, what with the face? One might think you are not happy."

"Aren't you going to hug me my love, I was really missing you!" said Rose.

Nestor didn't know what to say, let alone what to do. He went towards them while Leonora remained in the same position. She didn't utter a word. She didn't move. Sebastian came in her direction, hugged her and said:

"How beautiful you look my niece! A little too thin, but very beautiful. Aren't you going to talk to your uncle? Didn't you miss me?"

Leonora was still quiet—she didn't stop looking at Rose and Nestor. Rose feeling the weight of her stare, came closer to give her a hug. When Leonora realized it, she turned her back to everyone and left. Nestor was very disquieted and worried from the situation. He knew that Leonora wouldn't make their life easy while they were there, especially for Rose.

"Didn't you receive my last letter, my love? I wrote telling you we were coming."

"Yes, I did receive it, but there were so many things happening in the last few weeks that I completely forgot. What about you, sister-in-law, how have you been? So far you haven't said anything."

"I'm well, Nestor, but I feel that Leonora isn't. Her appearance is strange, her look then... Didn't you notice it, there was so much hate that it made me feel unwell."

"Don't pay attention, my love, she's always been like that. When something doesn't go to her liking, she behaves like that, with anger towards everyone," said Sebastian.

"Don't say that Sebastian, it's a lot more serious than what you think. We have been through very difficult moments. You cannot imagine what has been happening in this house."

"What do you mean? You told her about our marriage?" asked Rose.

"Yes, I told her, you don't want to know how she reacted, I just didn't manage to tell mother. The evening I was going to tell her everything was when the tragedy happened. Well, let's go inside, I'm expecting the priest for dinner."

Nestor went inside, ordered the servants to set more places at the table while Sebastian made himself comfortable with his wife and Nestor took Rose to his room. When Nestor went past Leonora's room he felt like knocking on the door, but thought better of it and gave up.

Father Gabriel had just arrived and Nestor went to meet him.

"Good evening father, so nice of you to accept my invitation."

"Good evening Nestor. I can see you're very anguished, child, what happened?"

"My brother has just arrived, bringing his wife and Rose, but it's not a good moment for them to be here."

"Why do you say that?"

"We'll talk after dinner, if you don't mind. The thing is, if we start now we'll be interrupted, for they are all coming down and our conversation has to be private."

"All right Nestor, we'll talk after dinner."

Father Gabriel enquired about Leonora and nobody knew what to say, when Nestor informed him:

"She's in her room, but she doesn't want to talk to anyone. I would very much appreciate it if you checked on her later."

Dinner was a calm affair, in spite of Nestor's tenseness. He wouldn't stop looking at the door—he had the impression that Leonora would turn up at any moment. They had tea in the sitting-room after dinner and then talked for a while, but Sebastian was very tired from the trip so he said good night and left. He called his wife, so they could rest together. Rose felt Nestor wanted to be alone with the priest and subtly followed her brother-in-law. She kissed her husband and went to bed.

"Could we go to the office father, we need to have a long conversation. I don't know where to start, nor how to tell you what I've been thinking—maybe you'll think I'm crazy."

"Don't worry, Nestor, tell me all your afflictions. I know more than you can imagine. I've seen a lot in this world."

"You know my past concerning the tragedy that had happened with the woman I loved the most in this life. I was still very young, but I really loved this woman. I never thought there could exist a feeling like what I had. You also know about her fateful death."

"Yes I do, you can skip this part, the Inquisitor confessed his crime before he died."

"Crime, father?"

"Yes child, because he knew that girl was innocent and he still sentenced her to death."

"God! How could he do such a thing—he was a priest!"

"Child, even priests make mistakes, we are like any of you, human beings."

"But why? What did Helen do to that man?"

"This I cannot tell you—the Inquisitor made a confession to me and for this reason I cannot say anything else."

Nestor was shocked by the revelation; he couldn't believe that a priest would send someone to be burnt at the stake, knowing they're innocent.

"Well, father, I've started to complete the puzzle since then. I'll tell you what happened in my family after the day Helen died."

Nestor tried not to forget any detail—saying everything he could remember, including all the circumstances from Leonora's changes, until the last dream she had.

"Nestor, we do have a case of reincarnation, only it was imposed by hatred, by the force of evil which Helen invoked at her time of death."

"Reincarnation? What are you saying? I don't understand."

"I'll leave you with some books, read them and you'll understand what I mean. What worries me the most is what the evil needed at that moment, something, a creature that was alive, so it could take root in the body and follow Helen's soul during her reincarnation. It would be with her while she lived because when she died her soul would have to belong to this evil."

"What do you mean? Forgive me father, but it is increasingly becoming more difficult to understand this. I've never believed in the devil, soul or ghosts. I did not know that everything is so complicated—it makes no sense to me."

"Believe me Nestor, both forces of good and evil exist and they have the same strength. In order for good to triumph over evil it's necessary to have an abundance of love. Only love can defeat the power of evil."

"Do you think that Leonora is possessed by the devil?"

"Not Leonora! She's Helen herself. Evil is near her, commanding her hate, and through it, Leonora changes, she's transformed, and forgets her good side, and allows the feeling of revenge to take over. I know it's hard to comprehend what I'm saying, but after you've read these books, you'll understand better."

"Tell me, though, what can we do to help Leonora?"

"We can all pray, and ask those who love Leonora and have loved her in this life to help her.

Only she can defeat the evil's force. If she cannot do it, her soul will be in evil's power for many, many centuries..."

"But it doesn't seem fair, she was innocent!"

"I know, my child, but Jesus died on the cross and forgave us, and that was why he sacrificed himself for us, so that we learnt how to forgive. I'll speak to Leonora now. Read all the books carefully, I'll be back at the end of the week—then we can talk about it in more depth."

"Pray for Leonora, father—she is very agitated with Rose's presence in this house."

"Nestor, talk to your wife, try to explain the situation and send her back to Paris, before it's too late."

"That's what I'll do father, I assure you. I don't know if she'll understand, but I'll try."

Father Gabriel left Nestor and knocked on Leonora's door.

"Leonora, it's me, the priest Gabriel, I'd like to talk to you, open the door, please!"

Leonora opened the door.

"Come in father, but please be brief, I'm not in the mood to talk."

Gabriel noticed the transformation, Leonora's eyes were enormous and shone in a strange way, her voice was heavy with hatred—she looked not at all like that fragile young woman, Leonora. Consequently, he spoke quickly:

"Helen, listen to me!"

Leonora turned to him, her eyes growing even bigger and as if throwing sparks, she replied:

"What did you call me? Helen?"

She laughed—her ironic laugh made her lips tremble.

"I'm not Helen, father. Even you decided to call me that?"

"You're Helen, and you know it. Right now you're her, but you're Leonora too. Choose, child, which one do you want to be in this life? There is no room for both; you have to make a choice: good or evil!"

Leonora's eyes at that moment transformed again, now they asked and begged for help.

"Child, I'll help you, but it's necessary that you make an effort to help yourself as well."

"How father? Tell me how! It's stronger than me, she's inside me."

"Leonora, she's you! What you have to do is to forgive all and yourself, let love take over your heart, that's the only way you'll defeat evil, with love. You've always been good to everyone. I know they made many mistakes, but forgive, they didn't know what they were doing; ignorance and fear made them blind to the terrible harm they were doing to you."

"It was her father, the cause of everything. They killed my family, my father, my mother and my youngest brother, they tortured them to death, they burnt me alive—no one had mercy on my soul, why would I have mercy on them now?"

"Well, because you learned how to love them! When you came to this family you had the opportunity to love and forgive."

"They took the man I loved away from me and want to do it again. I won't allow it! He wasn't there to save me, I called him many times and he didn't hear me. I won't forgive him for that, but now he'll be mine at any cost!"

"Shouldn't it be enough to know that he's suffered a lot for not arriving on time? Shouldn't it be enough to learn how much he loved you and still loves you to this date? You've partaken in his suffering for all these years, shouldn't that be enough? Child, they've all suffered a lot, they paid in life the evil they did to you. Don't you think you could forgive them?"

Gabriel managed to touch her heart, his words echoed in her mind.

"Actually, he's right," thought Leonora.

Leonora was quite taken by the priest's words and hadn't noticed that she had spoken as Helen and had remembered her past life.

"Have you noticed Leonora that you remember everything or almost everything related to your past life? Are you aware of what you just said?"

"Yes I am."

Leonora began to cry.

"My dream makes sense now."

"That's it Leonora, it will be easier now for you to learn how to control yourself, and not let the force of evil speak louder than your heart. Pray child for your soul to find peace and ask God to forgive your sins."

Father Gabriel left—Leonora was alone with her thoughts. Her wish was to run and call Nestor, she would like to tell him she was Helen, to see the look in his eyes when he found out she was the woman of his life…

Nestor waited for the priest. When Nestor saw him he ran to Father Gabriel on the stairs—he was distressed and wanted to know how Father Gabriel's conversation with Leonora went.

"Father, how was it?"

"Everything went well, Leonora is a lot calmer now, I don't know how long it will be like that, but I believe she is now more aware of everything that has happened to her."

"What did you talk about, is it ok for me to know?"

"Everything we talked in the office and a few more things. I'll tell you as soon as you've read the books. It'll be easier to understand. Now I need to go, I have a very early start tomorrow."

"Thank you very much, I'll ask the servant to take you back to the church."

Nestor was on his way to his room, but stopped in front of Leonora's room. He considered, for a few minutes, whether he should enter and talk to her or not. As if she could sense Nestor was there, standing, she got up and opened the door.

"Come in uncle, I really need to talk to you."

Leonora was cold with him, she wasn't nervous, but had a piercing look.

"I want Rose to go away—I don't wish to see her here. It'll be better for all of us. I ask you, make this woman leave!"

"Don't forget Leonora, this is her home too, we are mar…"

Leonora immediately interrupted what he was saying.

"I don't want to hear another word. Don't you complete what you were going to say. I'm giving a fair warning. I don't want any more tragedies taking place here—I need to be left in peace and with her here I won't be able to manage."

"You're still agitated; so, I won't take your threats into consideration. Besides, if she goes, I'll go."

"You wouldn't dare. Tell me you would have the courage to do that? Leave me here alone?"

"Tomorrow we'll talk more, for now let's sleep. I think you forget I'm your uncle, or rather, I'm more than that, I'm your…"

Once again Leonora interrupted what he was about to say.

"My love, the man that I love! That and nothing more than that!"

Nestor gave up, he wouldn't say anything else for tonight. He wished her goodnight and left the room. The day after, he talked to his brother and to Rose, asking them to return to Paris. He tried to explain, but it was very difficult for them to understand, for not even him knew exactly what to say.

Despite Nestor's request, Sebastian decided to stay for a few days. Every time they were in the garden,

Nestor looked at Leonora's window, and there she was, looking at both. Nestor had tried to get Leonora to leave her room, even Sebastian begged her to join them.

All the family wanted Leonora to be present to talk, but to no avail. She was afraid, she feared for her reaction, she didn't want to lose control, and she knew she would if she saw them both together.

So, Leonora stayed in her room reading the books the priest had left, fighting with all her might in order not to lose her emotional control. She struggled with herself the whole time against the feeling of hate.

When she saw both through the window, she ran inside and prayed, for she felt heat moving up her face, an uncontrollable attack of jealousy about to happen. She didn't know how long she would be able to stand this. She prayed, asking God to take Rose away from that home; she wouldn't be able to cope for much longer.

Nestor felt that Leonora was barely holding in her hate. He was very concerned and begged Rose to leave.

"Nestor, do you really want me to leave?"

"It's necessary, trust me, I know what I'm saying, please leave tomorrow."

"Are you sure this is not an excuse for you to be on your own with Leonora?"

"Please Rose, this is not a time for jealousy. It's bad enough having to put up with Leonora's! Not you too!"

"All right, I'll leave tomorrow, as you wish, but so far you haven't asked me what is so important that I have to tell you in person."

"It's true, you mentioned many times in your letters, I had forgotten. Forgive me."

"Let's go to your room, I'll tell you there. I'd like to be alone with you, my love."

While they walked to Nestor's room, Leonora's cat scratched the window asking to come in.

"Your runaway cat, where have you been all this time? I've been calling you!"

The cat curled up on her lap and Leonora stroked it. Then it jumped and moved to the bedroom's entrance. It scratched the door to leave and looked at Leonora in a beckoning way. Full of curiosity, Leonora followed in its direction and opened the door very slowly. Then, she looked down the corridor, to be sure there was no one around.

"Where would you like to go?"

At this moment, the cat walked towards Nestor's room. Leonora followed it. The cat stopped and looked at her. When she came closer to the door to pick it up and leave, she overheard the conversation between Nestor and Rose.

"All right, Rose, what's the secret, come on, tell me!"

"Darling, I want to tell you're going to be a dad!"

God is always by our side in moments like these—difficult times for Nestor and Leonora. He sent Gabriel, who with his sensitivity and knowledge of spiritual laws could bring clarification to so much pain.

This understanding comes with divine help so both could better comprehend their feelings and in some way help them in choosing the right path to follow.

But new situations were unraveling in the wheel of life, putting both face to face with a new extreme test.

Chapter 8 - Love's Redemption

Leonora certainly did not expect this blow. It was as if an arrow had crossed her heart—the pain she felt muffled the cry that came from her throat. She didn't know what to do, if she should run, if she should enter the room to spoil that moment of happiness, or if she should ignore what she had just learnt. Those Rose's words echoed in her mind. It was too much pain to bear so she let out a groan, which Nestor heard.

"What was that noise"?

"What noise?" answered Rose.

"A groan, as if someone were in pain."

"I didn't hear anything. I think it was your imagination. You are very tense and need to calm down."

"I'm thrilled to be a father! You have no idea how I've dreamt about this moment!"

"It's wonderful, my darling…"

Rose gave Nestor a big kiss.

Leonora couldn't listen to another word, she had to leave. She gathered all of her strength and left for her bedroom. She threw herself on her bed and started to cry. Her pain was such that she had not noticed that she had succeeded in dominating her hate. She was strong enough to suffer without hating.

In her despair Leonora prayed, calling everyone to come to her aid, as she wasn't sure how she could cope. In an instant, it seemed that her control over her anger would falter, but it was as if a voice came from within, saying:

"Pray, my child, ask God to enlighten your path."

So, for the first time, Leonora did manage to control herself. She battled her internal demons. She spent the rest of the night locked in her room. After a few hours, the fatigue won Leonora and she slept. It soon became dawn, as she tossed and turned, very agitated, as if she was having a nightmare. She groaned, cried, and was covered in sweat.

Nestor couldn't sleep and was going past Leonora's bedroom when he heard her groans. He entered her room very slowly when he saw Leonora tossing and turning, calling for him. His heart was completely split at that moment, but on seeing her all his doubts vanished. His love for her spoke louder, he would like to leave and do nothing, but it wasn't an option, he had to wake her up. He couldn't leave Leonora in that state.

"Wake up my angel… it's me, Nestor."

Nestor gently stroked her face, trying to wipe away the sweat. He moved her hair away from her face and called her name. As if coming out of a deep nightmare, Leonora opened her eyes. On seeing him, she slowly changed her gaze, becoming Helen again. Nestor soon noticed her transformation and tried to get away from her, but couldn't, she held his arm, and with great despair in her eyes, said:

"Don't leave me, please don't do this to me! I'm the one for you… don't let them separate us again, as they have done before."

Nestor tried to free himself from her arms, but he wasn't strong enough. His heart was racing, that woman still dominated him. As if she knew of her power, Helen or Leonora, put her lips over his and forced a kiss. It was a kiss that hurt, as it was so full of passion and pain at the same time. Their bodies interlaced and trembled together.

All Nestor could think was how two people could love each other so deeply; how was it possible to separate both if their souls were only one?

At that moment, Rose, who noticed her husband's absence, got up to look for him. As she passed Leonora's bedroom, she saw the door ajar and decided to go inside.

As Rose entered, she could not believe her eyes. Nestor was lying down next to Leonora and kissing her. Her shock was as deep as Leonora's when Leonora had learned that Nestor would be a father. Rose left running, and shut the door behind her. The surprise he felt with the sudden jar of the door shutting caused Nestor to immediately get up to check on who had just left.

At this moment, a scream was heard by the whole household. Rose had tripped over something as she ran away, causing her to roll down the stairs. The commotion woke everybody up. Very frightened, Sebastian and his wife went to see what had happened and were presented with one more tragic scene. Nestor held Rose's head, which had a trickle of blood running down her mouth. He was desperately screaming her name.

"In the name of God! Rose, talk to me! Don't die, please!"

Leonora, who saw everything from the top of the stairs, picked up her cat before anyone spotted it and sent it outside. Then, she stood there, observing Rose and Nestor, not knowing whether to feel sorry or happy. Sebastian was frightened. He looked at the scene while his wife called her sister. They were all in shock and she screamed pointing at Leonora's direction:

"It was Leonora! She killed my sister!"

She was beyond herself. Sebastian asked her to be quiet, not to repeat such an absurdity, but she wouldn't obey him, she screamed louder and louder:

"Murderer! You did it!"

"No, don't blame me, I was in my room, ask Uncle Nestor."

Sebastian and his wife looked at Nestor, as if expecting some explanation. What was he doing in his niece's bedroom that late? What had happened, after all, for Rose to fall down the stairs? Nestor was in no state to answer any questions—he held his wife on his lap and ordered the servants to fetch the doctor. It was actually too late, Rose was dead.

Two weeks passed, Sebastian was in the garden talking to Nestor.

"We need to leave, are you going to be okay here with Leonora?"

"I will, brother, I prefer you to go, I'll feel more relieved knowing that you're in Paris."

"Nestor, answer me, what were you doing in Leonora's bedroom that night?"

"I went in to check on what was going on— Leonora was moaning when I went past her room."

"Is that all? Didn't anything else happen?"

"No, Sebastian! I believe that Rose became frightened by something and so tumbled down the stairs."

"My wife cannot accept it—she accuses Leonora of her death and says that you know it was her."

"It's not true—Leonora has nothing to do with it. I was with her when we heard Rose's scream. The truth is Sebastian that this house is cursed. Since the day Helen died at the stake burned alive, strange things started to happen here. I still don't know the connection, but I'll find out. Father Gabriel has been helping me. We've been putting the facts together and will find the answer for everything that happened, but I prefer that no one lives in the house except for Leonora and me."

"You are right, strange things have happened since then. I believe it's better to take my wife away from here, but please, don't hesitate to call if you need me."

"I will—rest assured."

"I'm very sorry Nestor for you and your unborn child, and for Rose as well. It was a stupid death and hard to accept."

"Let's not talk about this. When are you leaving?"

"Tomorrow, first thing—I'd like to talk to Leonora before leaving, but I am afraid that she won't answer my knocks on her door and she won't leave her bedroom."

"She needs to be alone, she feels guilty for what happened, even though she wasn't to blame. She believes she contributed to the tragedy somehow."

"I won't insist on seeing Leonora, tell her that I believe her and am sending a big hug."

Next morning Sebastian left for Paris together with his wife. Leonora observed their departure from her bedroom window. She was deeply saddened by everything, especially by Nestor's pain. She knew how hurt he was with the death of his wife and unborn child. He longed to be a father.

Leonora didn't understand what had happened. She had no doubt that in spite of hating Rose, that she had done nothing to cause Rose's accident—she was even able to dominate her anger on that day. She was very confused and kept questioning herself. She talked to herself, or to a spirit, in hopes that the spirit would tell her who had killed Rose.

During the whole week Leonora prayed a lot for Rose's soul, she begged forgiveness for the hate she felt when she found out Rose was going to have Nestor's baby, and she talked with her guardian angel, Father Bartholomew.

During the day of Sebastian's departure, Nestor and Leonora hadn't seen each other. In the afternoon, she decided to leave the room and walk in the garden; she had been locked up in her room for far too long. She needed a bit of fresh air, but only now that everyone had left did she have the courage to do so.

In that moment of tranquility, Leonora looked at the flowers—breathed deeply to smell their perfume and felt a peace she hadn't felt for a long time. The air was light. She looked at the sky and noticed the shade of blue that day. Everything conspired so that Leonora felt good.

A gentle breeze blew in her face. She opened her eyes, as if she could feel someone's presence. It was then that she saw the image of Isabel and Louiza walking in the garden. She was paralyzed for a few seconds, when the two of them looked in her direction and pointed to the storehouse. Leonora looked on, not able to understand what they meant.

"What is it, Aunt Louiza? What are you trying to tell me?"

"That's where it lives—you need to finish with it."

On saying that, they started to vanish, until they disappeared completely.

Leonora was left with a heavy feeling, about something she needed to discover, but didn't know what it was, she felt a tightening in her chest. She decided to enter when she saw Father Gabriel had just arrived and was walking in her direction.

"Good afternoon, Leonora, how have you been, despite everything?"

"Well father, I know you were here last week and had a long conversation with Uncle Nestor."

"It's true, I was trying to console him—he was very disturbed by the tragedy. We talked a lot about the world of spirits and he told me he has read almost all the books I lent him."

"So have I, father, I have already read all of them and I'm very grateful for the books, which have been very useful to me."

"Where is Nestor? I'd like to talk to both of you together."

"I don't know, father, I'll ask the servants, hold on, I'll be back in a second."

Meanwhile Father Gabriel sat down underneath a heavily blooming tree. As he admired how beautiful it was, he saw Elizabeth. Father Gabriel had never had a psychic experience while awake, only when he was asleep. It was quite scary and deeply emotional, and he tried to control itself, managing to ask:

"What is it, my child, what is troubling your soul?"

Elizabeth's spirit cried excessively, calling Nestor.

"I'll pray for you, Elizabeth, I hope you find peace and that one day you can talk to your son."

Father Gabriel became very distraught with the vision. He had always known of people who had experienced this, but never imagined it could be so real. He thanked God for the grace. He was meditating in that peaceful moment when he heard Nestor's voice.

"We're here, father, I've been waiting for you the whole week. I've just finished reading the books you lent me."

"That's excellent. Tell me, what did you think? What's your opinion? Do you have any doubt?"

Both sat down next to the priest and Nestor spoke:

"Everything is very strange, but I really enjoyed the books. I believe they explain well everything that has happened in our lives and especially here in this home. Tell me, father, do you believe that Leonora really is Helen?"

Father Gabriel looked at Leonora and answered:

"I believe it's best that Leonora answers this question. What do you think, child?"

"Yes I am, father, I just don't know when I'm Helen. It happens without my noticing or being aware, everything is beyond my control."

"What else makes you sure you are her?"

"It's the love I feel for Nestor. It's stronger than any feeling I've ever known in this world, only Helen could love him so intensely."

While she spoke about her love, Nestor and the priest could again see her transformation. They had no more doubt that Helen and Leonora were the same person. Nestor felt hypnotized looking at her—his eyes became full of tears by the certainty he was talking to the woman of his dreams.

"Helen, my love, I never abandoned you. You have no idea how much I've suffered trying to arrive here on time, how much I've been suffering for loving you and missing you. I could never imagine you could be so close, although whenever I was by your side, since you were a child, I had a funny feeling."

Leonora and Nestor embraced, trying to control their emotion. Father Gabriel, who observed everything, became emotional seeing how they loved each other. He didn't want to interrupt that scene of pure and sincere love, but he needed to continue talking.

"There is something that really worries me a lot. Do you remember Nestor, when I talked about my doubt of how the demon keeps on taking over Helen?"

"Yes, I do, but I don't know how we can help you."

"Leonora will have to remember, she will have to find out where this malign force comes from so we can control it."

"Father, I don't know, I believe it is inside me."

"No, my child, what's inside you is hate, which is getting weaker as you have forgiven your grandmother. You told me that from your heart, on the day of her burial."

"It's true, father. When I think about her I don't feel any hate, I just miss her."

"Why did Leonora hate my mother?"

When father Gabriel was about to answer, he took his hand to his heart. He felt a sharp pain in his chest which turned his face pale. At that moment, he looked in the storehouse's direction, as if he had seen something that had frightened him. He wanted to breathe and talk, but had no time and gave his last whisper, dying in Nestor's arms. Leonora and Nestor didn't know what to do. They were left with no understanding of what had taken place. It was the most meaningless death they had ever witnessed.

Nestor called the family's doctor, who after examining Father Gabriel confirmed that he had died of a heart attack. Nestor and Leonora could no longer stand so many deaths; they were tired of having to deal with the feeling of loss. They were very shocked with Father Gabriel's death and the circumstances behind its occurrence.

It was one more mysterious death, exactly when they were coming to the conclusion of how to get rid of the malign force which commanded Leonora. Leonora, for her turn, was visibly sad with what had happened, feeling lost, with no direction. She didn't know how to solve her problem. She would have to find out on her own how to conquer the evil.

Some days had gone past. It was a Sunday afternoon and the day announced the arrival of a storm, the air was quite heavy. Nestor was in his office writing a letter to his brother telling him the latest news, when Leonora entered the room with a worried expression.

"What happened? You don't look like yourself" said Nestor.

"I'm not sure. I feel a tightening in my heart, as if something is about to happen."

The sky was black, with black clouds, and a strong wind started to blow, making the windows and doors slam shut. Nestor stood up and proceeded to close them, while Leonora tied the doors. Lightning blazed a trail through the sky and thunder made the house shake. Even the servants were scared. The oldest ones remembered the day when Leonora was born— the youngest ones had never seen such a storm. The impression was that the world was about to end.

Leonora was terrified, at each thunder clap she scrunched up like a scared child. Nestor tried to calm her but wasn't successful. Her body trembled from fear. Memories of a similar storm came to mind. She couldn't remember when she had seen anything similar.

At that moment, like flashes in her mind, Leonora saw a scene with people, walking from one side to another, brought a dead child in their arms and she didn't have any pity, didn't even want to have a look, just wanted to see the girl, the one who was alive: that's the one she wanted. During these thoughts she nodded her head as if saying no. Nestor noticed that something was happening to Leonora. He tried to call her back, but she didn't seem to hear anything.

She continued to have visions of the storm and didn't stop nodding with her head. She could see a poor woman on her bed, asking them not to take her daughter away. She tried to take the daughter from someone's arms, who Leonora could not distinguish as human; it looked more like a very large feline. She saw it with a black shadow which took the child, while the distressed woman died from grief.

"It was my mother! Nestor, it killed my mother!"

"Who? Talk to me Leonora, you're having another hallucination."

"The demon, when it took me from my mother's arms. She fought hard before she died."

"And where did it take you?"

"I don't know, I believe inside your home maybe in Isabel's room. Yes, was there... I see grandmother. I hate Elizabeth! It was her!"

Leonora started to shout Elizabeth's name, saying it with so much hate that Nestor was terrified with what could happen. She was dominated by the evil.

"God help me! I don't know what to do!"

Such was his despair that even the spirits had compassion for his soul—a soul that had suffered so much for his loved one who was taken by an evil spirit—that they came to his aid.

Nestor felt the blood drain from his face on seeing Isabel and Louiza enter his office followed by a priest. They were outlined in light—allowing Nestor to see more clearly their shape. He entered a state of ecstasy. He had never imagined he would see a spirit in his lifetime, and now he could see three at the same time. He was speechless, his legs frozen, until he heard the voice of his beloved sister Louiza.

"Take it easy, brother. You called us, so here we are. No need to be afraid, this physical phenomenon that allows you to see us, is called materialization [2]. We're here with the help of our brother Bartholomew, an old friend of Helen's."

Feeling sentimental, Nestor managed to speak:

"Sister, I missed you so much! How much I've prayed, begging for your forgiveness..."

"Well, Nestor, there was nothing to forgive you for, now that I comprehend what destiny is. I can now understand that nothing or no one can interfere in someone else's life."

Brother Bartholomew interrupted her:

"We have to help Leonora!"

She was still in a trance, thrashing around as if she were in an immense internal struggle. The spirit of Brother Bartholomew approached her and called:

---

[2] *Materialization* "...for the spirit whether the person is alive or dead, ..., can become visible and tangible." Allan Kardec, *The Mediums' Book* (Brazil: Federação Espírita Brasileira, 1986) 126, Chapter VII: From Bi-Corporeality and Transfiguration, question 114.

"Helen, my child, please listen to me."

At that moment, on hearing her name and Bartholomew's voice, Helen stopped shaking her head, waiting to hear what he had to say.

"Pay attention, my child! Make an effort and try to remember the moment of your death, go back to the past…"

Then, Bartholomew put his hand in the direction of her forehead, which made a ray of light go through Leonora.

At this moment, she started to scream:

"No, I don't want to remember, it hurts too much… Bartholomew, don't ask me that!"

"It is very important Helen—I promise you, you won't feel the pain. You know very well that everything is gone, it's only a memory from the past."

Leonora slowly calmed down, and called for Nestor, as she was scared. In her mind the image of the burning fire made her heart beat faster.

"Calm down!" said Bartholomew. "Be very calm, nothing is actually happening. It's only some recollection in your memory."

"I'm looking at everybody at the square. I hate them. There are people laughing, I'm going to kill them, I swear I am!"

"Helen, you had your revenge on the real culprits, forget about this hate, you don't hate anyone else. I want you to pay attention to your own words and see the moment when this evil force took you over."

"I'll have my revenge."

Leonora spoke as if she were reliving her death.

"I swear I'll be back! I will take my revenge on all of you! I'm looking at the Inquisitor and her... How I hate her! I will haunt her! Even if I have to invoke the devil's power to do so..."

Her tone of voice demonstrated such great despair that Nestor, during her narration saw everything in his mind. Suddenly, Leonora, semi-conscious, said:

"I can remember Bartholomew—I invoked the demon at that moment, my heart died down, only my mind was alive."

"Pay attention now, my child, who or what do you see at this moment?"

Gradually, as if her memory slowly came back, and trying to remember, she said:

"My cat! It's there, that's my cat!"

"The cat!" exclaimed Nestor.

"It's the cat—why didn't I think about it before?"

"We all knew, my child, but it wasn't up to us to say it—it was necessary for Leonora to recall. It's she who can defeat it, no one else, these recollections will make her see that the evil is in it. There would be no point in us telling her, she's the one who needed to be sure that her cat was the one bringing evil, and using its body to be always near her."

"And now, Father Bartholomew, what will happen to Leonora?"

"Child, never forget my words. The divine will be made! Due to her hatred, Helen took away many lives. Even though she was impelled by the force of evil, she does have her share of responsibility; she'll have a substantial debt to all of these souls. Therefore, pray and ask God to enlighten your beloved, as she still isn't totally free from this evil. As I have already said, only love can defeat it."

Bartholomew put his hand again on Leonora's forehead, making her return to herself. Feeling very tired, Leonora looked in disbelief at Bartholomew and said:

"My guardian angel, you are here?! But how?"

"Yes, my child, I came to help you and I want you to remember everything that happened."

Once again, he stroked Leonora's forehead, making her remember everything. Nestor was by her side, holding her hand.

"Leonora, look who's here." said Nestor.

She looked at Nestor and was amazed at how he could also see spirits.

"Yes, I can also see them, Leonora, thanks to Father Gabriel, who taught me a lot about this subject."

Bartholomew added:

"Seeing Leonora's suffering made you more sensitive and understanding—it made your heart accept the facts with more love. Suffering purifies the soul. That's why we all have to suffer in our lives, some more, some less, according to the burden we need to carry."

Isabel and Louiza, who hadn't said a word so far, approached Nestor:

"Be ready, brother. Soon we'll bring someone to talk to you."

The three spiritual siblings said their goodbyes, wishing both the strength to continue their lives, that God have mercy on them and that they never lose faith.

After they faded away, Nestor kept staring at the emptiness; he was astonished by what had just happened. He looked at Leonora as if he wanted her confirmation that everything had been real, not a dream. Leonora, who was used to those occurrences, answered positively, without him having to ask.

"Let's sleep, Leonora, we're very tired. Tomorrow we'll talk about everything and we will look for the cat."

"I don't want to look for it, I'm scared."

"Let's not talk about it now, come on."

Nestor took Leonora in his arms, feeling she was debilitated. He put her to bed, kissed her gently on the face and went to his bedroom. The storm had stopped for a while, but the sky was still dark with clouds, as if it was still going to rain. Nestor closed all the windows, including those in Leonora's room. He locked them tight, as he didn't want the wind to open them, and above all else, for the cat not to come in.

After that, Nestor went to his bedroom thinking how he would find the cat and destroy it. He could not let Leonora solve such a difficult problem on her own, even knowing only she could defeat the cat.

Meanwhile, in her bedroom Leonora couldn't stop thinking about what she'd just discovered. Despite knowing that her cat had been possessed, she could not be angry at it, let alone want to kill it. She thought about the nights they spent together, when she was alone in her room, feeling lonely, abandoned by everybody; all the moments she talked to it and it understood like no other. She knew that her heart wouldn't feel hate anymore, so there was no longer danger, the cat was only protecting its owner.

Leonora was trying to find excuses for it, as if she wanted to forgive it. The cat wasn't to blame for everything, it didn't deserve to die.

Next morning Nestor got up very early. He had hardly slept, having suffered a restless night. He was about to have breakfast when Leonora, who had hardly slept as well, turned up at the dining room. Her face was calm, with a serene appearance. She wore a blue-turquoise dress, her favorite color and she wore her hair loose. She came very close to Nestor, who, on smelling her perfume, turned around and said:

"I can smell your perfume, darling, you cannot surprise me."

"Good morning, Nestor. You look tired— didn't you have a goodnight sleep?"

"I could hardly sleep. I kept thinking how we can find the cat. Do you know how?"

"No. It's the one to turn up at my bedroom, it's always been this way. I've never looked for it. Whenever I needed help, as if the cat knew it, it came to me."

"We need to find where it hides."

"But uncle, is that really necessary, aren't we exaggerating?"

"How do you mean, have you forgotten everything that happened yesterday, Leonora? I have no doubt, this cat is possessed. We mustn't doubt that."

"You're right, but it's hard for me to believe it, it's always been so good to me."

"Well, let's finish our breakfast so we can go and search for it."

So that's what they did. They searched every corner in the garden. They went to the cowshed and couldn't find anything. Leonora called it, but nothing, not a single meow.

"Well, I think it knows we're searching for it, and I'm sure it won't turn up."

"Quite probably. If it has a pact with the devil, it won't let us get hold of it so easily."

They decided to sit underneath a tree to rest for a while. Leonora lay on the grass and put her head on Nestor's lap, while he stroked her hair which fell on his legs in the shape of a waterfall. The world could end at that moment—the peace they felt was almost a miracle: they could have never imagined they could one day enjoy this moment.

The silence let them hear the voice of their hearts, which beat with such serenity, allowing both souls to be free of any curse for a short time, as if it was a truce from the gods.

Nestor closed his eyes, imagining how good it would be if it was all a bad dream and that Helen was alive by his side. He remembered the time in which both stayed together in the field for hours, sitting under a tree, and let time pass by without anyone disturbing that moment of love and peace.

That was exactly what Nestor felt now with Leonora, as if he had gone back in time. He didn't want to open his eyes. He was afraid everything was going to end, it was so good, he wouldn't open his eyes ever again. He would like to stop time in that moment of peace and happiness. He was reflecting, lost in his thoughts, when he heard a voice coming from very, very far…

"Nestor my son, I miss you so much. Open your eyes, I'm here!"

Unable to believe his ears, he opened his eyes slowly.

"Mother, you came!"

Leonora, who was awake, looked at him. She was scared as she didn't see Elizabeth's spirit.

"Dear mother, how are you?"

"Son, let me talk, I'm still very tired, I haven't been able to rest yet. I need you to forgive me for the evil I caused all of you, especially the two of you, but I want you to know that I was and I am very regretful of everything. Son, in order for my spirit to have peace, I need your forgiveness, and Leonora's as well."

"Mother, I don't understand, I have nothing to forgive you!"

"Yes you do, my son. I brought misfortune to your and Helen's lives. Now, listen to me: take the Inquisitor's letter, read it and you'll understand... and, if you can, my son, forgive me."

Without another word, Elizabeth's spirit, with the help of Isabel's and Louiza's spirits, went away. Nestor couldn't move for some time, he could hardly hear Leonora, who was calling him.

"Uncle Nestor, talk to me, what's going on?"

"Leonora, I've just talked to your grandmother, didn't you see her?"

"No, I heard you say her name, I knew you were talking to her, but I couldn't see anything."

"She asked for our forgiveness. She said she'll only have peace when we forgive her."

"I've forgiven my grandma for a long time, since the day of her death. Brother Bartholomew made me understand everything that had happened and made me feel love for her."

"I don't know what she's done, but she asked me to get the Inquisitor's letter."

"Go Nestor, get the letter, read it and forgive her as I've already done."

Nestor got up and walked towards the house, leaving Leonora on her own; he asked to go alone. His steps were heavy, his heart told him he was going to find out something that would make him very sad, but he had to face the problem in order to finish with this suffering once and for all.

Wasting no more time, Nestor went to his desk got the bundle of letters and proceeded to search for it and open it when he found it. His heart was pounding, he had a premonition that it was time he found out the whole truth.

"Dear friend Elizabeth, I hereby come to clarify to you and to myself all the fateful events which have taken place since the day we made the greatest mistake of our lives. I want you to know that I leave this world carrying a great burden in my conscience, because I know and have always known that Helen was innocent.

All my present suffering is nothing compared to what I've done. I know, dear Elizabeth, that you're going to suffer as much as, or even more, than I. You know very well what we've done, be aware my friend, that we were the cause of so much evil… because of vanity, pride and prejudice we convicted that poor child to death, with fraudulent evidence so that she could be condemned as a witch. Besides that, I tortured the whole family to death.

God forgive me—power made me blind and in its name I tortured innocent people and sent others to their death.

Since that day I've never forgotten Helen's eyes in the square. While her body was on fire, her eyes fixated on us. There was so much hate that only the Devil could have given them so much strength to resist the fire, being left intact.

Elizabeth, I want you to know and that you try to help your grandchild. She's possessed by Helen's soul. She was the one present at the church on the day of the accident. She was at the window and commanded the candle with the power of her eyes. I saw it at that exact moment.

Her cat is the devil incarnate and it commands Helen's soul. Seek help, a priest who is also an exorcist. That'll be the only way you'll avoid any more tragedies in your family. She's not going to stop, only when she's destroyed everyone. May God forgive you and me, because we're to blame for everything.

I depart from this world, to a cursed one. Pray for me, if you have a chance. Help my soul, as it'll be in the hands of the Devil."

Nestor couldn't see the letter anymore—his eyes were full of tears. Like a child, he cried, sobbed, calling for Helen… He found it very difficult to accept that his mother caused Helen's death.

"Why, Lord? Why my mother? What harm had Helen done? It's hard to believe it."

Nestor couldn't stop crying, and he begged Helen for forgiveness the whole time, as if he was the one to blame. Exactly at that moment Leonora came in, or rather, Helen, as she had changed, her deep and big eyes looked at the man she loved so much. Seeing him so disquieted from finding out the truth, her voice was gentle and full of compassion.

"Stop it, I've already forgiven Elizabeth, there is no need to be like that."

"I can't Helen, you were only a child, what harm did you do to them to deserve such evil?"

"I didn't do anything, I only loved you. It was enough for your mother, as she would never accept her son married to a peasant."

"I cannot believe that this was the reason for such an atrocity."

She came close to him, held his face with both her hands, forcing him to look at her.

"How I've been suffering, only to think that someone would separate us again. My hatred stemmed from the fear of losing you. I didn't have any intention of killing anyone, but I could not accept the idea that they could tear us apart."

"Helen, I love you so much! I really want you! Let's depart from here forever. Let's leave to a place far away where we can forget our past and live happily. We have this right, after all they took this chance away from us. Let's run away from everything and from all the ghosts that follow us."

"My love, I've waited so long for this moment."

Their lips locked in such a passionate kiss, with so much anguish and desire that there could not be anyone witness to what would happen to both. After years of longing and suffering, they would make love, with desperation and passion so that nothing else could prevent that moment. Not even the ghosts could interrupt them. Exhausted from the intensity of their love making, tiredness made them fall asleep in each other's arms.

"I'm in your arms, held tight, never to leave again..." that was what Leonora was thinking before she fell asleep.

If there were witnesses to that moment, they certainly would be jealous. Not even the angels could ignore such deep love.

The sun was rising, promising a beautiful morning, when they were woken up by a noise coming from the hallway.

"Where are you Nestor? Still asleep? You're not like you used to be, waking up at the crack of dawn? Brother, I've arrived!"

Nestor didn't even have time to get up, when his bedroom door was opened. Sebastian's shock was etched on his face. He did not want to believe his eyes… his niece in bed with her uncle!

"I can't believe! You must be crazy my brother!"

"Calm down, Sebastian, don't rush to any conclusions, we'll talk later."

Sebastian was appalled.

"Get off this bed right now, Leonora! Your mother would turn in her grave. This is simply outrageous. Didn't you hear what I said, girl? Leave right now!"

Leonora looked at Nestor waiting for an answer, but the most he did was to look at his brother, thinking about the best way to talk with him, in order to avoid another tragedy.

"I won't leave, only if Nestor tells me to, you can't make me do it!"

"Your impertinent child, everybody was right, you bewitched Nestor—he never would have done this. They were right, only I didn't want to see it."

"Shut up Sebastian! You don't know what you're saying!"

Leonora's eyes were already full of hatred, her voice became stronger and more aggressive, as if the anger she felt for all in that family was springing again from the past. On hearing his niece's impertinence, he went towards the bed to remove her from there. At this moment, Nestor held his arm tight and said:

"Don't do that my brother. Go downstairs and wait for me. We'll talk in the cold light of day."

Feeling upset about everything, Sebastian left to the living room to wait for Nestor. Disgusted by the situation, he thought of Rose's accident, drawing a hasty conclusion of what she might have seen that night in his niece's room.

Leonora was quite agitated, her appearance had already changed, she paced up and down the bedroom, while Nestor attempted to calm her down.

"Don't be like this, darling, I'll talk to him, everything will sort out, you'll see!"

"Nestor, he'll want to separate us, I can't allow that!"

"Don't behave like that. Please Leonora, don't let hatred take over you. Everything is fine, no one will separate us, that's a promise."

"Did you look in Sebastian's eyes? Did you see his look of disdain, as if I was someone vulgar? I can't abide such treatment. I cannot tolerate people looking at me as if they feel superior."

"Don't pay any attention, Sebastian was only taken by surprise. We have to admit it's difficult for people to understand our love, don't forget they're used to seeing us as father and daughter. I'll talk to him. Now please my dear, go get changed, have your breakfast, and read something, everything will be all right."

Nestor kissed Leonora, stroked her face, and looked at her as if asking for her to be calm, and went to meet his brother. Upon arriving in the hall, he found Sebastian standing, looking out the window, arms crossed, moving his body—clearly showing his impatience and indignation with what he had just witnessed.

"Now I understand why I couldn't stop thinking of returning to this house. My heart was warning me that something very wrong was happening here."

"It was a bad decision to come back—you don't know anything to judge so quickly."

"What do you want me to understand? That you're having an affair with your niece, or rather, that she's your lover? Don't you have a heavy conscience because of Rose's death, or are you going to try to deceive me again, telling me that your wife didn't see anything that night?"

"If you continue talking in that manner I won't be able to explain what's been happening, and please, talk quietly, I don't want Leonora to hear our conversation."

"Are you scared of her, brother? Do you believe she has a pact with the Devil?"

Sebastian was screaming. Leonora could hear everything, even if she didn't want to, it would have been impossible. He was talking so loud everybody could hear, including the servants.

Leonora came down the stairs, and stayed behind the door to better hear and understand what the brothers were saying. She didn't want Sebastian to convince Nestor that he was doing something wrong in staying with her. She would have to do something to constrain Sebastian and she certainly would stop him in if necessary.

"Sebastian, I know it's hard to understand what was happening... but I ask you, let's have our breakfast in peace. We'll talk somewhere else, believe me, brother. I know what I'm doing. And... I'm not afraid of Leonora, but I fear for you. Please, don't talk anymore about this subject for now."

Sebastian tried to calm himself down when he heard Nestor's appeal. He had to give his brother a vote of confidence, after all he had always been the responsible one in the family—he couldn't have completely taken leave of his senses. They had breakfast together, not uttering a single word.

Leonora returned to her room, she was quite anxious about the conversation they were about to have. She'd find a way to listen to it. Sebastian and Nestor, walked to the garden, while Leonora followed them from her window and she saw when they went in the direction of the storehouse. On opening the door of the small building Nestor had shivers run down his spine and he even had a fright.

"What's the matter?" Sebastian asked.

"I had a bad feeling when I opened the door. Didn't you feel it? It was as if a draft passed by."

Sebastian looked at his brother—he could hardly believe what he had just heard.

"I believe that you have become very superstitious. You never talked like this before... but now all you talk about is spirits, the force of evil, you don't seem to be the same person."

"Believe it brother, all of this does exist, I experienced it myself—a short while ago I spoke to the spirit of our mother."

Sebastian gave him a half smile, teasing him.

"I believe this is all an excuse for yourself. You don't fool me."

"I need you to believe me. Can't you understand? Come, I'll tell you the whole story, with all the details, later you can tell me whether I was right or wrong!"

Meanwhile Leonora left her room to go to the storehouse. She was very agitated—any threat was a reason for her to become unhinged. Her fear of losing Nestor was so immense, that seeing someone in the family was enough for her to believe she ran that risk.

On the way, Leonora passed by some servants —they looked at her with fear. They could feel something on her that frightened them; so they lowered their heads afraid of facing her. They were terrified of her look. They all felt that Leonora wasn't alone. They had been at that house long enough to know that something really bad was about to take place. Instinctively, they moved away from her. They let her go past and did the sign of the cross straight after.

Nestor told Sebastian everything, and tried not to leave anything out. He listened without interrupting, and waited for the end of the story to express himself.

"Then my brother that's everything. I've just told you the whole truth about what happened in our family over the last few years. As you can see, Leonora is not guilty of anything."

"How not? Are you so blind you can't see how much she is guilty? Aren't you forgetting the death of our parents, our sisters and even your wife and unborn child? Nestor, you're bewitched by this woman, she's a witch! Mother was right when she denounced her, but the evidence is here: Leonora is part of the Devil. She killed almost our entire family, there are only the two of us left, can't you see it? She's going to kill us too."

Sebastian was becoming agitated, spoke loudly, and was gesticulating energetically. Leonora went to the small window in the storehouse. She could hardly see as the window was so small, but it was enough for her to observe everything and imagine what they were saying.

"You have to finish with her Nestor, before it's too late—she has killed us one by one."

"No!" screamed Nestor. "You haven't understood anything I've said!"

"I have my brother, you're the one who's sick. I need to take you from here as fast as I can—I won't leave you alone with Leonora again."

"Stop! Don't say anything else!"

Sebastian wouldn't stop talking—he had lost control of himself. The atmosphere was very heavy. It seemed that they were fighting, as Sebastian shook his brother in the hope of making him wake up.

At that moment, the shadow of a cat jumped on top of Sebastian. The brothers tried to catch it, but it ran away from one side to another, distracting them from the fact that a fire was starting to spread out on the wooden floor. Leonora, who saw everything, knocked on the door, but it was locked. She shouted at it to open it.

When Nestor and Sebastian came to realize what was happening, they were already surrounded by the fire. The brothers tried to leave but they couldn't get anywhere near the door. Outside Leonora screamed for help. No servant had the courage to check on what was happening at the storehouse. They were too scared and feigned that they couldn't hear her.

Desperately, Leonora said aloud that nothing could happen to Nestor, she asked the cat for help, but it stayed on the roof, looking at her. At that point she could hear the voice of evil, coming from it, saying:

"They all have to die, don't forget that Helen, the Werck family has to disappear. This was your promise of revenge, now you'll have to fulfill it until the end."

Soon after these words, a demonic laugh came from the depths of hell. Sobbing, Leonora still tried to talk it out of killing Nestor, when she remembered Bartholomew's words.

"Only love will defeat the force of evil..." thought Leonora.

"Don't let Nestor die, I beg you! I'll do anything, but he can't die!"

Through the small window Nestor could see Leonora screaming his name. Trying to survive he smashed the glass to release the smoke from the building and to breathe. But it was too late, Sebastian couldn't breathe anymore. Desperately, Nestor still tried to save Sebastian by taking him closer to the window.

Still screaming hopelessly, Leonora asked her cat:

"Help Nestor, do you hear? I don't want him to die!"

Leonora ran from one side to another, not knowing what to do, she was completely desperate. Her fear of fire dazed her and she couldn't act. At that moment, she heard Bartholomew talking to her:

"Leonora, my child, only love will defeat evil, only you have the power to destroy it."

Then Leonora asked Bartholomew for strength and help, and also prayed that God forgive her for all mistakes. When she looked one more time inside the storehouse she saw her love almost fainting and Sebastian catching on fire. Her love spoke louder than any curse or fear.

In that moment of despair and pain, Leonora ran to the door, gathered all the strength she possessed at that moment and managed to break it. Not thinking about the fire, she entered the place calling for Nestor, who couldn't talk anymore. Almost fainting, he could only drag himself closer to her.

With all the love Leonora felt for Nestor she asked God to save him, as she would die in his place. At that moment, with the help of the angels, she took Nestor's hand, dragging him outside. Suddenly the cat jumped on her lap trying to prevent her from saving him—it even scratched her.

The storehouse was about to explode because of all the ammunition and weapons that were inside. Then Leonora quickly got hold of the cat and entered the burning place again, locking the door behind her. In a matter of seconds Leonora had her body burning and felt hallucinating pain over her entire body.

"I'll kill you. It's over. I don't want any more revenge and you're going to die with me."

The cat fought, trying to be free from her arms, as she cursed it:

"You'll never cause any harm to anyone ever again. If I've made you incarnate from the darkness, I'll make you die and go back to your place."

Leonora cried in pain, as the fire had already spread all over her body. She called God to come and help her, and not let the evil take away her soul. There was a flash of light with the explosion. Nestor, who had just recovered and was still on the floor looked in disbelief at the new tragedy.

"Leonora! No!"

It was too late, everything was over.

The pain Nestor felt at that moment came from the depths of his soul. He wouldn't be able to deal with the loss of his love once again. He wept so desperately that all around took pity on him. His distressful roars of pain were so loud they woken even the dead. He cried for Helen's name and the whole garden seemed to shake as if somehow she was going to appear in front of him. He continued to crazily scream, saying once again he couldn't save her…

"Helen, my love, I failed again. How will I be able to live without you?"

Nobody managed to get near Nestor. The servants extinguished the fire and prayed at the same time for that desperate soul, who couldn't accept losing the love of his life again.

Nestor resembled a zombie. One week after the accident he was still immobile. The spirits tried to help him without any success; he refused to believe in anything he heard. He stayed locked in his bedroom, just calling for Helen.

His sister-in-law arrived at the Werck's castle. She had received the sad news and was in complete shock. In the letter the servant told her about Nestor's pitiful state. With nothing else to be done, she decided to go to the cursed place, to bring him back to Paris with her. Her desolation was clear to see due to Sebastian's death. She was pale and thin, but brought something within her that gave her strength to fight for life.

"How are you Nestor? Once again I return to this house with a lot of pain in my heart. I hope, brother-in-law, never to set my foot here again."

"You can be sure you won't" he said.

Nestor was barely audible. He called all servants, and in the presence of them, announced that they were being laid off. The ones who had been there for a long while would receive a settlement so they wouldn't need to work again. He thanked all for their hard work, their honesty and dedication to the Werck family.

Then Nestor handed all the paperwork of possessions, deeds and titles to his sister-in-law, informing her of the contents of the whole estate.

"Nestor, I don't understand what you're trying to do. You're giving me your whole fortune, including your share?"

"I just won't give you the deed to this house, as it'll die with me."

"How come, what do you mean?"

"Dear sister-in-law, I have no reason to live, I carry a very heavy burden on my shoulders. As much as I believe in God, I fear he gave me a heavier weight than I can carry."

"Don't say that, Nestor. It's blasphemy. God knows you can handle it; otherwise he wouldn't give you this load. Believe me, Nestor, you'll have his help! And if that isn't enough, maybe the news I have will help. I'm pregnant, Sebastian's baby's here, inside me."

"I'm so glad, and I'm sure my brother's soul is happy in knowing that our family isn't finished, that this child will give continuity to our family name."

"You're alive, brother-in-law, you shouldn't talk like that!"

"No, I'm dead. There's nothing left inside me. What you see in front of you is only matter, because my soul left when Leonora died to save me. Now, sister-in-law, go! Don't look back, be happy and in peace. Make your child love our surname and be proud you're resuscitating the ashes of the Werck family. May you use this name to help all that one day knock at your door asking for help, that it can correct all the mistakes we made in our past, so that in spirit we can be proud of having one day been part of this family."

They said their goodbyes, not to meet again in this life. At least that's what Nestor imagined. A few hours later he was outside the house, watching it being consumed by fire. While he watched, hoping that everything would disappear, he thought about his mother.

"Mother, I hope that you are in peace, for I have already forgiven you. Please ask God to forgive me."

Nestor mounted his horse and rode in the direction of the grotto. Having not been there for such a long period of time, the entrance was hidden by some undergrowth. He walked slowly through the dense bushes until he arrived where the vegetation allowed his entrance.

He could feel the silence of the place penetrating his being. He directed himself to the stone altar, went down on his knees and moved some small rocks and residue away which hid a small box. It was buried there many years ago. A weak light illuminated his face, and at the center of the altar, he saw the spirit of Brother Bartholomew.

"Nestor, I know nothing I say right now will change your decision, but I'll still say it. Don't do this! This is not the way for you to be together forever. God gave us life and only God can take it away. You'll create a negative karma for your soul. Be resigned to your fate and wait for the Divine Law—it'll tell you when your souls can finally reunite forever."

On saying that, Bartholomew disappeared, leaving Nestor very confused by his words, but he was still determined to go ahead with what he had planned. He left the grotto carrying the small box and rode to the cliff next to the castle.

As Nestor arrived he dismounted and walked slowly till he was standing right at the edge; below choppy waters hit the rocks with force. At that moment, he looked at the horizon, opened the box and let the wind carry the ashes of the woman he had so much loved in his life.

Filled with hope in his heart and determined to find and reunite with Helen's spirit, Nestor closed his eyes, raised his arms as if preparing for a long flight and called his lover's name:

"Helen, wait for me!"

A profound silence took over the place, the wind, so strong, sounded like a lament coming from a crying soul.

Thus it ends in this life the tragic saga of two souls who loved each other deeply, and even after death, will continue to love each other, and for all eternity they'll fight for this love...

Life goes on and the characters in this drama will return for new experiences, new learning, and for the redemption of their personal karmas.

A New Life Starts Again...

Ten years had gone past, and in the garden of a beautiful mansion in Paris, two children walked hand in hand. Their mother observed the scene and was very proud to see how much they liked each other—how her son looked after and cared for his sister, despite being the exact same age, as they were twins.

Both were by the main gate when the girl turned to her brother and asked:

"What does Werck mean?"

"It is our surname, we come from an old traditional family, and our mission is to preserve our history."

The girl looked at her brother, and said:

"I love you brother."

"Me too, sister."

The End

The Curse of the Werck Family
Eternal Souls

The continuation of the Wercks' saga will be published in the next book of the series:

The Curse of the Werck Family

Volume II: Eternal Souls

In this book, the main characters in this drama come back to life in fascinating Paris as brother and sister.

France, 1539: Life moves fast in flamboyant Paris, after the mysterious and tragic death of the Wercks' ancestors, in the land south of the kingdom. The curse of the Werck family is renewed with the birth of the twins Bárbara and Leonardo—souls reborn in this life united by a great love.

Throughout this story, the twins re-connect with friends and enemies so that through this new relationship they might have more opportunities to learn and forgive—encounters which raise profound feelings of hate, love, jealousy, passion, faith and resignation.

Unforeseen events unleash a series of investigations into the lives of the Werck family—investigations that lead back to the time of the Inquisition, witches, and fires, taking the characters from this drama to new discoveries, and surprising scenes and circumstances.

Unexpected and impressive turn of events happen along this intense and involving romantic saga, where the situations presented by the wheel of life direct the destiny of each of those involved, bringing moments of happiness, pain, despair and suffering, which end up chiseling their spirits...

Until the siblings can manage to find peace and finally find... companionship love, friendship love, maternal love, compassionate love, eternal love... of

Eternal Souls...

About the Author

The author was born into a spiritual family, in the city of Rio de Janeiro, Brazil. From an early age, due to her extreme sensitivity, she has been in contact with the spiritual world. Throughout her existence, with the help of her spirit friends, she has developed her psychic abilities—learning how to use this gift to benefit others. In the year of 1998, she was inspired by the spirit Andorra, using her psychographics and clairvoyance abilities, to write her first romance.

The responsibility of the spiritual work is enormous and for this reason, "I hope to continue to be deserving of the gift of receiving stories that talk about life and death, trying in some way to help those who go through hardships, giving them patience, understanding and resignation. Along these years, I've had many experiences with my spiritual friends, so I'm very grateful for all this time we've been together and united in the happiness of serving for the good of all."

About the Publisher

Piu Book is a publishing house that publishes books which touch hearts, inspire lives and open consciousness, so we can spread the seeds to a better world.

Words of Love, Seeds of Light!!!

To learn more about the publisher…

Visit our site
www.piubook.com

Like our pages on
www.facebook.com/piubook
www.instagram.com/piubook
www.twitter.com/@piubook

Talk to us by our e-mail
pb@piubook.com